ISAAC ASIMOV'S
ROBOTS IN TIME

by
WILLIAM F. WU

THE LAWS OF ROBOTICS

1.

A robot may not injure a human being, or through inaction, allow a human being to come to harm.

2.

A robot must obey the orders given it by human beings except where such orders would conflict with the First Law.

3.

A robot must protect its own existence as long as such protection does not conflict with the First or Second Law.

Don't Miss the Next Exciting Adventure in
ISAAC ASIMOV'S ROBOTS IN TIME *Series*
by William F. Wu
Coming Soon from Avon Books

MARAUDER

ISAAC ASIMOV'S
ROBOTS
IN TIME™

PREDATOR

WILLIAM F. WU

Databank by Matt Elson

A Byron Preiss Book

AVON BOOKS • NEW YORK

ISAAC ASIMOV'S ROBOTS IN TIME: PREDATOR is an original
publication of Avon Books. This work has never before appeared in
book form. This work is a novel. Any similarity to actual persons
or events is purely coincidental.
An Isaac Asimov's Robot City book.
Special thanks to Janet Asimov, John Betancourt, Leigh Grossman,
John Douglas, and Chris Miller.

AVON BOOKS
A division of
The Hearst Corporation
1350 Avenue of the Americas
New York, New York 10019

First AvoNova Printing: April 1993

AVONOVA TRADEMARK REG. U.S. PAT. OFF. AND IN OTHER COUNTRIES,
MARCA REGISTRADA, HECHO EN U.S.A.

Printed in the U.S.A.

RA   10 9 8 7 6 5 4 3 2 1

This novel is dedicated to

Bill Moss,

*in memory of all those colorful plastic dinosaurs
we used to play with,
and of our formative years together.*

Special thanks are due for help in writing this novel to Michael D. Toman, as usual, for invaluable research aid; Dr. William Q. Wu and Cecile F. Wu, my parents, for indulging my childhood interest in dinosaurs; Ricia Mainhardt; John Betancourt; and Byron Preiss.

Foreword

In "Robot Visions," Dr. Isaac Asimov writes about a question inherent in any time travel story—whether individuals traveling in time will alter events that would have occurred without the interference of a time traveler. Most writers who tackle this question write about changing the past and whether doing so is desirable or not. The Good Doctor, once again exhibiting the originality of his own vision, chooses to focus on a more rarely examined concern: of traveling into the future, and the possible consequences of doing so.

Stories that merely take place in the future are not the same as stories about individuals who travel from their own time, whatever it is, to their future. To my knowledge, the first science fiction novel to tell such a story is the classic novel by H. G. Wells, *The Time Machine*. In it Wells writes of a man who travels to the distant future from Victorian England, the time and place in which Wells was writing the novel. However, Wells presented a dystopian vision of the future as a warning of what could happen if the rigid social and economic divisions of his own society worsened to the extreme. The possibility of avoiding that vision lay not with the time traveler, but with the people who lived in Wells's time. Wells did not really examine whether his time traveler's report to his friends back in his own time would bring about a different future.

Two theories of history influence the tale any writer tells about time travel. One belief is that only large forces such as technological advance, economic change, and the development of religions and philosophies determine the direction of history. The other theory is that any event, no matter how small, sends out ripples of influence that profoundly affect all other events. An historian told me that his colleagues are about evenly divided in their support of these theories. Authors of time travel stories always write with one or the other implicit, if not explicit, in their work.

I first discovered the science fiction of Isaac Asimov as a child and have read both his fiction and nonfiction in the years since then. Writing time travel stories about his positronic robots and his Three Laws of Robotics is therefore a special honor for me, and I hope you will enjoy the *Robots in Time* series. By way of introduction, this book presents the late Dr. Asimov's fantastic "Robot Visions."

William F. Wu.

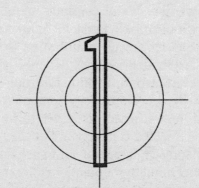

Mojave Center Governor sat in his office, deep in the underground city of Mojave Center. He was an experimental humaniform robot of a type that was new this year, 2140. Each of the Governor robots was currently running all the municipal systems of one entire, newly-constructed city. They were doing so under probationary status, monitored by a committee of scientists through their computer.

His office was in the middle level of the city, in the center of that level. He didn't really need an office at all since most of his work was done through his radio link to the city computer or directly to municipal departments; further, he could plug into various terminals when necessary. However, he had learned that humans sometimes preferred doing business in an office, so he maintained a small room in Mojave Center for that purpose.

At the moment, MC Governor was alone. He plugged his humaniform forefinger into a wall jack. Inside the jack, the end of his finger opened and plugged into the system. He contacted the city computer.

"I am going to run a simulation program again," said MC Governor. "I will continue my normal duties through my multi-tasking system. However, I instruct you not to transfer any communication or other interruption lower than Priority 5. When I have finished running the simulation, I will notify you."

"Acknowledged," said the city computer.

MC Governor returned his finger to human shape, breaking the shielded connection. For the sake of security, he told himself, he chose not to use radio communication concerning the simulation programs. Lately he had been running them more often than before.

He ran down his list of programs. They were standard simulation programs that all the Governors used to discover and correct potential problems and challenges without actually having to face them in real life. His favorites involved some sort of disaster that befell Mojave Center, requiring him to respond urgently under the Laws of Robotics to restore the situation to normal. Like all positronic robots, he was programmed so that his greatest imperative, and his greatest reward, was in obeying the Laws. The First Law of Robotics was, "A robot may not injure a human being, or, through inaction, allow a human being to come to harm."

This time, he selected the program called Desert Flash Flood. It was essentially a form of role-playing game. He began running it. Suddenly he found himself standing in the main thoroughfare of Mojave Center, Antelope Valley Boulevard, with water a meter high pouring down the street.

MC Governor was a very tall, brawny robot. He ran through the water to a young woman who was stumbling and splashing helplessly, trying to hold a toddler in her arms. As MC Governor picked her up and strode through the current toward an escalator, he radioed the city monitors who controlled all the basic life functions.

"Shut down all electricity to nonessential services if they have failed to shut down automatically," he instructed the computer, as he carried the woman and her child. "Run a status check on the emergency electrical systems providing essential services."

Right now, his greatest worry was the electrocution of humans if broken power lines touched the flood water. As a Governor robot, he was a central control unit, capable of managing entire cities, from traffic to essential services and utilities, to environmental control and industry. The city had its own decentralized computer systems, which reported directly to him and took his instructions by way of his internal radio and video systems.

"Thank you," the woman gasped, clutching her drenched toddler as MC Governor set her down on the rising escalator.

Almost immediately, the monitors reported that nonessential services were being discontinued. The escalator stopped moving, but the woman stumbled on up the steps. MC Governor waded back into the water toward a trolley full of humans stranded on one side of the boulevard. They were yelling and screaming in panic. Its robot driver was speaking calmly to his passengers, asking for patience.

The city monitors reported that the emergency power system was functioning safely.

"Send me all data related to the cause of the flood," he ordered. At the same time, he moved behind the stranded vehicle. It normally ran on a battery-powered electric motor. Now the robot driver steered as MC Governor pushed the vehicle to the stationary escalator, where the driver began helping the humans onto it.

As the monitors all over the city reported their data, MC Governor computed the information. A flash flood had taken place in the Mojave Desert above them, washing down from the San Gabriel Mountains to the south. Normally, it should not have been a problem. The top surface of Mojave Center, a large rectangle on the desert floor, was comprised mostly of solar cells, which provided power. It was fully sealed, of course, so that flood water would normally pass right over the underground city. In this case, however, the force of the flood had ripped open the surface and water was still pouring down into the top levels of the city.

Robots working on those levels were already struggling to seal off the leak. Others all over the city were coordinating evacuation efforts for the humans. MC Governor was about to request the details of those efforts when he was interrupted from outside the simulation program.

"City computer calling Mojave Center Governor with a Priority 8 emergency."

MC Governor shut off the simulation and inserted his finger into the wall jack again to shield his communication. "MC Governor here. Report the emergency."

"Flooding is reported on the main level over Antelope Valley Boulevard. At this time, the Priority 8 emergency is estimated to be thirty-seven minutes from reaching a Priority 9 level without additional measures."

"What is the cause of the flooding?"

"The circulation of water was routed incorrectly through the city. Too much water was directed to the problem area, and the increased pressure burst two main valves simultaneously."

"Why was the water routed incorrectly?"

"The orders came from you."

"Are all standard emergency procedures under way?"

"Affirmative. The most critical is that all drainage systems are open to the maximum."

MC Governor quickly broke the connection and ran outside. The scene was similar to that of the simulation, though not identical. Not as much water was running down the boulevard; it was only half a meter deep, but many more people were running for the escalators and sliding ramps, yelling to each other. MC Governor was horrified; somehow, he had allowed his involvement with the simulation to influence his multi-tasking ability. Unwittingly, he had begun to create the flood in the simulation, putting humans at risk in violation of the First Law of Robotics.

He waded into the water, snatched up two children who had been knocked off their feet by the current, and carried them to the nearest rising slide ramp.

"City computer," he radioed. "What is the status of the broken valves now?"

"A robot maintenance team has shut off the water flow manually at the preceding valves. The broken valves are not yet under replacement."

Around MC Governor, people were still in danger. The shallow water would not drown anyone in the areas where it had flowed into gentle backwaters, but the current was powerful enough to knock people down.

If they were injured, they might drown even in shallow water. Other robots were already wading through the water, carrying people to safety.

A short, balding man with frizzy gray hair had lost his footing. Though sitting in water that was not over his head, he was clinging to the bumper of a small utility vehicle, unable to pull himself up against the force of the current. He pulled himself toward the bumper, tried to gain traction with his feet, and was knocked down again. This time he lost his grip and was rolled roughly down the boulevard.

MC Governor waded quickly to the man and lifted him up. He was an engineer named Max Eisen, to whom MC Governor had spoken briefly before. As MC Governor carried him, Eisen coughed and wheezed, but was breathing. In several long strides, MC Governor returned to the ramp, where he set the man down in a sitting position. Then he looked around again.

"Over there," Max wheezed, pointing.

A young woman with curly orange hair had jumped up onto the pedestal next to an abstract stone sculpture. She was looking doubtfully at the water swirling around the base of the pedestal. As MC Governor hurried toward her, the pedestal tilted from the imbalance her weight caused. Water flowed under its raised edge, pushing it over.

The young woman gasped as she was thrown through the air. The stone sculpture began to slide off its pedestal in the same direction. Before she hit the water, however, MC Governor managed to catch her and swing her out of the way. In the spot where she would have struck the water, the stone sculpture splashed and then cracked against the hard floor beneath it.

"You are safe now," said MC Governor, carrying her back to the ramp to join Max.

The water was slowing down quickly now. With the broken pipes turned off and the drainage open to the maximum, the emergency was passing. Up and down the boulevard, robots were helping humans to safety and seeing to their injuries if they had sustained any.

"Elaine," said Max. "I would like to introduce you to Mojave Center Governor, the robot who runs our city."

"Pleased to meet you." Elaine smiled gratefully, brushing her orange hair out of her face. "And thank you."

"I may not deserve thanks," MC Governor said grimly. "I should never have allowed this to happen."

Internally, he radioed the water system monitors again. They all reported good drainage. Then he called the city computer. "Are you aware of any immediate First Law imperatives that are not being addressed?"

"No."

"Compile total damage estimates, including human casualties, and relay them to me as soon as they are reasonably complete. Prioritize repairs according to safety factors." He was very worried that his lapse had caused humans to be injured or worse.

"Acknowledged," said the city computer.

Then MC Governor reviewed the power monitors and turned the electricity back on in all the branches of the system that were undamaged.

"Elaine just moved here," said Max. "I'm afraid this wasn't a very good introduction, Elaine, but Mojave Center really promises to be a good place to live."

MC Governor towered over Max as he looked down at him. "Do you need medical care? Either of you?"

"I'm okay," said Elaine, looking up at him with wide-eyed wonder. "Thanks to you and the First Law of Robotics."

"I twisted my ankle," said Max, shifting his weight. "I don't think it's too serious, but maybe it should be looked at."

"Of course."

"We shouldn't keep you," said Elaine. "I'm sure you should be in contact with all your subordinates."

"I am," said MC Governor. "My multi-tasking ability allows me to make contacts and decisions even as we speak." He lifted Max gently and began walking up the ramp. "Max, I will take you to the nearest first aid station."

"Okay."

Elaine walked with them. "Can I ask you another question? Why are you so *gigantic*?"

Max laughed.

"Actually, I am a gestalt robot. I am comprised of six robots, both in body and in mind."

"What?" She cocked her head to one side, puzzled. "You mean you can divide into six smaller robots?"

"Yes, that is right." MC Governor smiled. "The reason I am this big is that I can divide into six robots of rather small human stature, slender and short."

"But what for? Why not just make one big one, like you are, if that's what the city needs?"

"In the event of certain types of large-scale emergencies, I can divide into my component robots so that each can move directly to a different site to manage damage control."

"Makes sense to me," said Max. "Right, Elaine?"

"Yes, I see. But what about your brain, Governor? Does it segment somehow?"

"No, not physically." MC Governor was amused at the thought. "Their positronic brains are physically distinct from mine, of course, but right now all six are merging data with mine to create my own personality. In order to divide, I will have to allow each latent personality to separate and take control over its data as well as its own body."

"I'm impressed," said Elaine. "And a little confused. I never heard of anything like this—that is, a robot like you."

"He represents the new cutting edge in municipal robotics," said Max. "I read all about him. And this very moment, even as he speaks to us, he's also monitoring all the energy consumption, security matters, engineering functions, and anything else you can think of regarding the city."

"You're doing all that right now?" Elaine studied MC Governor's face, as though for a clue of some sort to the effort he was expending.

"That is the job." MC Governor shrugged amiably. "I was constructed for it, so to me, combining all these duties is not surprising."

"Tell me," said Elaine, studying his face curiously. "What do you do for fun?"

"Aw, I don't think robots have a lot of fun," said Max. "Uh, do they?"

"As a robot, my greatest pleasure is in obeying the Three Laws of Robotics. That value is hardwired into my positronic brain, as it is with all positronic robots." MC Governor smiled, enjoying the mere thought of them.

"The First Law of Robotics says, 'A robot may not injure a human being—' "

"Yes," said Elaine, nodding recognition. "We learned them in school."

MC Governor heard her, but he really wanted to recite them all. Doing so gave him a feeling of security and satisfaction. "The Second Law is, 'A robot must obey the orders given it by human beings except where such orders would conflict with the First Law.' Then the Third Law of Robotics is—"

" 'A robot must protect his own existence as long as such protection does not conflict with the First or Second Laws,' " Elaine finished, grinning impishly.

"Yes—exactly," said MC Governor, suddenly embarrassed. "Please pardon me for boring you with this matter." He was about to ask Elaine some polite questions about her interests when he received a radio alert from the city's communication center.

"Governor, Priority 6 communication is requested."

"Acknowledged," said MC Governor. Priority 6 also required a shielded communication, so he would have to take it in his office, but it was not enough to override his duty to Max. He delivered Max to the robots at a first aid station, bade both humans goodbye, and hurried toward his office.

As MC Governor strode quickly down Antelope Valley Boulevard toward one of the slidewalks, he judged the damage he could see. The underground city had different levels, connected by various moving ramps, slidewalks, and lifts; generally, they appeared untouched. Of course, much of the water damage would not be immediately visible.

As he walked, all he could think about was that he had failed in his duty.

MC Governor sat down in his desk chair and plugged his humaniform forefinger into a wall jack once more. He gave his password and called for the Priority 6 message.

"Message source: The Governor Robot Oversight Committee Computer.

"Text: The Governor Robots of the following experimental cities have entered closed loops: Emerald City, Republic of Ireland; Kenyatta Center, Kenya; New Monegaw Springs, Missouri; Osaka Center, Japan; Rio de Oro Center, Brazil."

The exact times that each Governor had entered the closed loop were given next. MC Governor adjusted those times for the different time zones in which each city was located around the world. He found that each Governor robot had malfunctioned within the last three hours.

MC Governor disconnected, his mind working quickly. He was one of only six Governor robots being tested on Earth right now, and the other five had all failed today. Since the Governors had all been constructed with the same basic design, he was forced to conclude that he would experience the same fate, probably very soon.

MC Governor had a very levelheaded, rational, not very flashy personality. He was totally dedicated to his job. However, when he was thinking alone, without having to pace himself to human abilities or to slower electronic equipment, he could think extremely quickly.

Now his own existence was threatened. Since neither a threat to humans nor direct human orders were present, the First and Second Laws of Robotics did not apply. Under these conditions, the Third Law of Robotics compelled him to evaluate his position at maximum efficiency in both speed and clarity.

Obviously, some crucial design flaw was about to make him enter a closed loop. It would put him into a state roughly parallel to a comatose condition in humans. Even worse, however, was the danger from the Oversight Committee of scientists.

In order to study him, they would have to dismantle him even if they could take control of him before he entered the closed loop. They would need nothing more than to reach him with a direct order for him to shut himself down until further notice; under the Second Law, their instruction alone would be enough to control his behavior. His first priority was to insulate himself from receiving any such instruction. After that, he would have to find out how to avoid entering the endless loop.

He was able to infer some information that was not actually part of the message. For instance, the message came from the Oversight Committee's computer, not the committee itself. Their computer had probably judged for itself that the message should be sent to him. So far the scientists had apparently not learned of this.

MC Governor did not know how often the scientists actually reviewed the data regarding the Governors. Since the experimental robots had already been functioning successfully for many months without a problem, the four roboticists were probably not bothering to check the data too frequently. However, an emergency of this magnitude would probably prompt their computer to contact their offices directly. When they learned that he had caused water mains to break by incorrectly routing the normal water supply, they would be even more concerned.

His deliberations and immediate plans were formed in less than a second. A more detailed strategy would have to wait until he had more information. First he plugged back into the secure link to the city computer.

"Priority 10," he instructed. That meant that only he or the scientists on the committee could access this. He had no way to prevent them from getting information from anywhere in the Mojave Center system, but he could stop accidental leaks of information. "Delete all records of receipt, storage, and acknowledgment of last Priority 6 message. Until further directives from me, indicate to all exterior and interior communications that city operations are functioning normally. Do not pass any direct instructions to me from any humans. Store them and use Priority 10 communication to tell me that some have arrived, without revealing their content."

When the city computer had acknowledged receipt, he withdrew his finger. That would delay any instructions from the Oversight Committee, but not for long. They would merely have to call any human here in Mojave Center and ask him to pass the orders on to MC Governor. If he stayed in his office, however, he would not have to hear any human instructions in person, either.

MC Governor plugged back into the city computer. "Priority 10. Have a detail of Security robots report to the exterior of my office immediately and block all humans from entering. The Security detail is to report to me if any humans approach my office. They are not to convey any direct messages of any kind to me from a human until and unless I personally give further instructions."

He hesitated, at least by robotic standards. If a human ordered a Security robot to convey a message, the Second Law would override his own orders. He would have to block that possibility with a First Law imperative.

"I, MC Governor, may be in personal danger from anticipated human contact. If my functions are disrupted, harm may come to the human residents of Mojave Center. A First Law imperative is therefore involved."

That would not stop the Oversight Committee's directives from reaching him forever, but it would be enough at least to force the Committee to make some effort. The robots on Security detail would have to be persuaded that a greater or more immediate First Law imperative overrode this one. Otherwise, they would have to be physically disabled or destroyed before they would disobey his instructions.

The danger of his entering an endless loop was more complex. He had never noticed any tendency on his part to enter any sort of long-term loop. If the scientists on the Oversight Committee had learned of this problem, he would have heard from them before now. That meant that the problem was likely to hit with no internal warning.

His own monitoring systems might not be reliable. He judged that his best chance to learn something quickly about his own basic design was to contact his creator, Wayne Nystrom. Wayne was not part of the Oversight Committee, of course, since its mission was to study his work. MC Governor would have to call him and instruct the city computer to shield the call and delete all records of it.

MC Governor did not want—in human terms—to die.

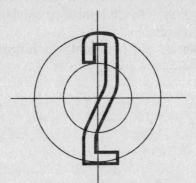

Wayne Nystrom stood inside his air-conditioned mobile office, looking out the window. In the distance, the turquoise waters of the Atlantic Ocean and the pale sand of the Florida beach were bright in the sunlight. Immediately in front of him, however, robot drivers were piling the sand in huge mounds with giant earth movers, preparing a place for Turquoise Coast, the latest underground city of Wayne's own design. Like the others, it would be run by a Governor robot that was still under construction.

"Biggest challenge yet," he muttered. He was alone in his office, as he always preferred. Eccentric and secure in the knowledge of his own brilliance, he preferred his own company to anyone else's and often carried out private conversations with himself, being the only human on any planet whom he really trusted. At the age of forty-one, he was finally achieving the success with his creations that he had always known he deserved.

His telephone beeped his personal code. He moved

toward it reluctantly, still watching the robot crew dig into the sand outside. "And they told me I couldn't build an underground city here because you strike water so soon under the surface," he growled sourly. "Wrong again, as usual."

He sighed and pushed the button on his telephone speaker. "Yeah?"

"Good day, Dr. Nystrom." The humaniform robot face of Mojave Center Governor came on the video screen.

"Hello, Governor!" Wayne instantly relaxed when he realized that the caller was one of his own robotic creations. "I'm glad to hear from you! How are you?"

"I have an emergency situation that I may not be able to handle," said MC Governor somberly.

"Not likely," said Wayne, though he welcomed the challenge of an intellectual puzzle. Besides, MC Governor had always been somber and serious. "What's the problem?"

"The Third Law prevents me from speaking of it by public telephone. I need help. Will you come to see me so that we can talk in private?"

"Of course," said Wayne. "I stand by all of my creations. You know that. Will tomorrow be soon enough?"

"I fear not," said MC Governor. "Every hour counts. Perhaps every minute."

Wayne hesitated, surprised. He was anxious to know more and was suddenly frightened by the sense of urgency that MC Governor was conveying. "All right. This project doesn't need me right now. I'll arrange a flight right away."

MC Governor disconnected, unsure whether Dr. Nystrom could really help him. While Dr. Nystrom might be the only one who could enlighten him quickly on his basic design flaw, his creator might simply arrive too late.

Dr. Nystrom would first have to pack and arrange a chartered SST flight from Florida to Mojave Center's small airport. That would take some time, as would the flight itself. If nothing unexpected occurred to slow him down, he needed a couple of hours to get here at absolute minimum.

MC Governor decided to review his internal data. He began by examining his design in three-dimensional blueprint, but he saw nothing he had not seen before. Then he began running the standard simulation programs.

All the simulations presented options that involved the Three Laws of Robotics. As he reviewed them, he ran short segments of each, looking for irregularities. These simulations were as close to a hobby as he possessed.

MC Governor especially liked the simulations that presented him with First Law imperatives. In fact, they were the part of his programming that kept his morale high. He opened his favorite one, Earthquake Simulation 9, near the climax.

In this one, a major earthquake has shaken the San Andreas Fault, roughly seventy kilometers west of Mojave Center. Because of the danger of earthquakes in the region, Mojave Center had been designed and constructed as a self-contained, sealed unit. Its four sides and floor were sealed, the surfaces smooth and the edges rounded. Theoretically, it would float in the sand around it during an earthquake of virtually any magnitude, with its water tanks and batteries safely inside.

During a major quake, the box containing the city would be shaken, mostly laterally, snapping off the aqueducts that brought water down from the mountaintops in the area. The solar panels on the top surface, however, would remain attached and functional. When the quake stopped, the city should remain intact, though the floating might bring it to rest at a slightly tilted angle.

Inside the city, of course, all the positronic robot labor would be warning humans to stay inside and helping them find secure locations.

However, Earthquake Simulation 9 postulated an additional problem. After a simulated earthquake of nine on the Richter scale, Mojave Center has survived intact but has come to rest at a severe angle. The robots can adjust their perception of spatial relations more easily than humans, and the human residents are disoriented and near hysteria.

Then a major aftershock hits. Now that the city is no longer in its original position, and has already sustained major stress to its outer shell, it is much more vulnerable, and parts of the city begin to break. At this point, MC Governor decided to turn on the simulation.

In MC Governor's positronic imagination, he strode through Antelope Valley Boulevard against four feet of rushing water. It flowed out of broken water pipes protruding from the walls and poured down all the streets.

"City computer," MC Governor ordered in quick, firm tones through the radio link. "Shut down all electricity in Mojave Center now. Trigger all emergency chemical lights immediately. Priority 1, First Law emergency in effect."

Instantly, the normal bright, indirect electric light

went off, to be replaced by slightly dimmer orange and yellow light sources provided by chemical reactions. They were in self-contained, waterproof units that would not, if broken, endanger humans by sending an electrical charge into the water. Meanwhile, helpless humans screamed and clung to whatever railings or fixed furnishings they could, in danger of drowning or being dashed against the walls, debris, and malfunctioning ramps and escalators.

As MC Governor passed, he picked them up in his strong arms as though they were children, holding them high above the dangerous water. "You will be taken to safety," he said calmly. "Please do not struggle."

Respecting his judgment and ability, the frightened humans obeyed him.

All around him, other robots were also rescuing humans from imminent death and severe injury wherever they could. Still more robots used tools or their own robotic body strength to close valves or crimp pipes shut in whatever way was possible. Driven by the First Law, every robot present was risking his own existence to save the humans.

With a woman sitting on his shoulders and two grown men under each arm, MC Governor forced his way to an upper level where an escalator was still functioning. He could have just set them down and let them find their way to the surface, but his interpretation of the First Law would not allow that. Instead, he climbed up the moving escalator, still carrying his charges.

On the top level, which was devoted entirely to engineering, MC Governor set down his human burden in temporary safety. Then he reached up to manipulate the controls of an emergency exit. It was a trapdoor that operated on springs instead of electricity so that it could still be used in moments such as this. He threw it open with a clang and led the three humans out into the fresh, dry air of the Mojave Desert, where, blinking and squinting in the bright sunlight, they stumbled onto the shiny solar panels that lay on the top of the city.

"Remain here," said MC Governor. "Stay on the sand, away from the top surface of Mojave Center. The open sand will be safe in the event that additional aftershocks take place."

They nodded and moved away from the solar panels that marked the top of the city.

MC Governor saw that they were safe and leaped back down through the trapdoor. Shouting and also sending a Priority 1 radio signal to all the robots, he announced that he had opened an escape route and described its location. As the other robots began directing and carrying humans to safety on the surface, he ran back down to pick up as many more of the injured and panicked humans as he could find.

MC Governor ran the simulation through to its conclusion, saving many lives by repeatedly carrying and leading humans to safety. The simulation ended when all the human survivors had been rescued. Then, deeply satisfied with the feeling of accomplishment in following a long, complex series of First Law imperatives, he turned it off.

As a routine matter, he checked the passage of time—and was astounded. He usually ran through a simulation in no more than fifteen to thirty seconds; even accounting for the time he had spent checking segments of other simulations, he had expected to find a total time usage of no more than forty seconds. Instead, he had used two minutes and six seconds. While the time itself was not significant, the extent of his miscalculation was alarming.

"First clue I have found of something wrong," he said to himself. "This kind of malfunction is rare for a positronic brain." He decided to call up the times he had spent on simulations during the past week.

What he found was even more worrisome. Each occasion had taken more time than the one before, and he had not previously noticed that. Also, the curve was rising sharply. He had spent two minutes, six seconds this time; one minute, twenty-one seconds the previous incident; fifty-nine seconds before that. These simulations had been run during the last twelve hours. Before these, the times were all in the normal range, from thirty to forty-five seconds.

"This may be it. The problem I have been looking for. If I can figure out exactly what it is."

MC Governor usually checked the time of all his activities, as a matter of routine. After running each of these simulations, he should have noticed the unusual times, but he had not. Of course, at that time, he had not been alerted to the possibility of a significant flaw in his design, so the increases had not seemed important.

Now they did.

He began calculating an extrapolation of his recent behavior with the simulations. This included the simulations he had chosen, their characteristics, and the length of time he had spent on each one. It took very little time.

When MC Governor had finished his calculations, he knew that he was in serious trouble. The length of time he was spending running each simulation was rising so rapidly that at the existing rate, he would do nothing else in only a few more hours. That was consistent with his meager information about the fate of the other Governor robots.

The cause he had found was even more serious. By sifting through all the simulations available, and examining those that he had been selecting more and more frequently, he had isolated a handful of them that all possessed the same flaw. Each of the bad simulations was improperly triggering his response to the Three Laws of Robotics, enhancing his devotion to them out of proportion to the fact that these were merely simulated experiences.

Because of this flaw in the simulation programs, all the Governor robots eventually would find a scenario in which they would be obeying all Three Laws of Robotics to the utmost. They would experience a virtual robot's Utopia. Since a robot's only pleasure came from obeying the Three Laws of Robotics, this simulation would provide a kind of perpetual high, almost like that of drug addiction.

Since the other Governors had already entered closed loops, MC Governor estimated that the simulation was just as addictive to robots as certain drugs were to humans.

The process was simple, involving three stages of addiction. First, any Governor running the flawed simulation programs would devote more and more of his time and energy to these simulations. This was where MC Governor stood now.

Second, the Governor robot would spend all his time in simulations, still running the city simultaneously with his multi-tasking abilities. In the final stage, his flow of orders and actions would slow drastically, impairing the execution of his normal duties. As the program went into an endless loop and brought all other thoughts to a halt, he would ultimately shut himself down.

"I have not reached that point yet," MC Governor said inwardly. "But even now I can feel the craving to run another simulation. I have predicted my own destruction."

The Third Law of Robotics would not allow him to sit passively and wait for that destruction, however.

MC Governor checked his monitors for a routine review of the city. As usual, everything was running fine. Then he took another step toward shielding himself.

First he shut down all incoming communication except his emergency line. That would prevent any chance of his thoughts accidentally mixing with a link to the city or another robot. His efforts to escape the endless loop and subsequent dismantling by investigating roboticists would require leaving as slight a trail as possible.

"I see one chance," MC Governor decided. The six component humaniform robots comprising him could not run the simulation individually. "So if I divide—if they split up—they are in no danger of the addiction. I will not exist in this current form, but I will have obeyed the Third Law by preserving all my component parts and their data."

The problem did not end there, however. The six component robots could not run the city of Mojave Center after they had separated. They would still have all of MC Governor's data and communication devices, but that would not be enough for them to do his job.

The information from the various monitors that were physically located within their bodies normally flowed to the gestalt consciousness of the Governor. That consciousness would cease to exist when the Governor divided, leaving the data nowhere to combine and the city computer and sensors nowhere to send their signals.

"I will not be able to function in this job, either in my gestalt form or in a divided form." MC Governor knew that he still faced imminent destruction.

Naturally, once the Governor was no longer running the city, the Oversight Committee monitoring the experiment would want to know why. To find out, they would dismantle all the component robots, effectively killing the Governor. So the Third Law still required that he take more steps to save them.

"They must flee," MC Governor decided. "Each one separately, wherever he chooses to go. Like the other Governors, I will have failed my field test, but the Oversight Committee can arrange for older models of robots to run the city."

An alert reached him through his emergency line. According to his recent instructions, it conveyed no other information. Worried, he plugged his finger back into the cable jack and gave his password.

"Messages have arrived for you, Governor," reported the city computer.

"Give me the sources," said MC Governor. "No actual messages."

"Two from the Oversight Committee computer, one from Dr. Redfield of that committee."

"Priorities?"

"The first two are Priority 6. The last is Priority 10."

MC Governor disconnected. He had very little time left.

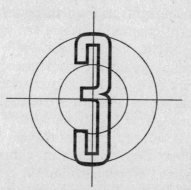

MC Governor made an internal shift in his programming. He activated the six positronic brains of the component robots. They were sharing his data already, but they would need to join in the deliberations he was making. Since they all had different specialties, they also had distinct personalities. The seven-way discussion was conducted through internal signals.

"Where would you flee under this Third Law imperative?" MC Governor asked them.

"We must be careful not to go anywhere that would endanger humans," MC 1 warned.

"Obviously," said MC 2. "We all know the Laws as well as you."

"My specialty is the environmental impact of Mojave Center on the surrounding desert," said MC 1. "I can tell all of you that finding a place on Earth where we will not disturb anyone will be difficult."

"You know I am the troubleshooter for this city," said MC 2. "I find that there is always a solution of some kind to a problem."

"Stay focused on the subject, please," MC Governor said sternly. "We do not have much time. Now, clearly the First Law prevents us from disrupting others. The other pertinent question is, where can we hide effectively? We—that is, the six of you—will be fugitives. Your chances of getting on board spacecraft to leave the planet are poor. So are your chances of evading capture if you stay on this planet. MC 3, you specialize in city Security. What is your appraisal?"

"To robots, 'security' requires that we avoid receiving instructions from any human. Otherwise, under the Second Law, virtually any human can capture us just by ordering us to cooperate with him. However, I believe we can avoid hearing any instructions."

"How?" MC Governor asked. He was feeling a stronger desire than ever before to run one of those simulation programs again. The addiction was increasing its power over him.

"Mojave Center has a new generation of miniaturization unit in its Bohung Medical Research Institute. These are most often used to reduce robots and equipment to microscopic size so that they can work on humans by traveling through the bloodstream."

"This is nothing new," said MC Governor. "The principle is quite old, in fact."

"Our new unit can do far more than earlier types," said MC 3. "As before, a shower of subatomic particles alters the molecular structure of the subject, yet allows the subject to retain its shape and functions. The equipment itself will not shrink. Only we will. The difference—"

"This is a start," said MC 4. "But if we are still

within the hearing of human instructions, we can be apprehended under the Second Law, even if we are too small to be seen."

"Allow MC 3 to finish," ordered MC Governor.

"The difference," MC 3 continued angrily, "is that this unit is theoretically capable of using the same system to create time travel."

For the first time, MC Governor felt an energy surge of excitement. "Really? How can this work?"

"Some simple modifications in the miniaturization equipment will alter the character of the device. As a time travel gate, it also showers the traveler with sub-atomic particles. Chaos theory in physics has established that a certain percentage of the particles will move out of time, as in experiments involving the Heisenberg uncertainty principle; in sufficient combination, they will create a funnel into the past. When that funnel is large enough, it will take anything within its cone back to a certain point in time. If we are microscopic at the time, we can be taken."

"How much control do we have over where we go?" MC 6, the city specialist in social stability, was programmed to be cautious.

"We should have precise control, based on the precision of the machine and its equipment," said MC 3. "Remembering, of course, that this has never actually been attempted."

"So a Third Law danger exists," said MC 6. "But that is overridden by the imperatives of the First and Second Laws, which might be well served."

"If you go back to any point in time before the positronic brain was invented," said MC Governor, "none of the humans around you will have heard of the Three Laws of Robotics. So they would never try to control you with orders under the Second Law."

"If they saw us, they might tell us what to do mistaking us for humans," said MC 4. "We would still have to obey them, even if they did not know we are robots."

"The danger would be changing the past," said MC Governor. "Anything you did back in time, especially in relation to significant historical events, could violate the First Law by altering the course of history."

"We cannot take that risk," said MC 3. "In the very act of interacting with other humans, we would come across First Law imperatives in our immediate surroundings. We would have to act, and in doing so, we would be changing history."

"Exactly," said MC Governor.

"We can avoid that problem," MC 3 added. "The combination of miniaturization and time travel should eliminate it."

"That should work," said MC 5. "I understand. First we miniaturize to microscopic level. Then we go back into the past. Once there, we will be too small to perceive First Law imperatives and no humans will give us any instructions because they will not know we exist."

"It sounds acceptable to me," said MC Governor. "Does anyone see a flaw in this logic?"

None of the robots answered immediately. MC Governor waited patiently. Then, one by one, each of them agreed that this appeared to be an acceptable course of action.

"Does anyone have another plan that will satisfy the Laws of Robotics to an equal degree and entail less risk?" MC Governor asked.

Another robotic pause followed. Again, each of the six

gradually concluded that this was the best plan that the group could devise. MC Governor concurred.

"Then we must get to the miniaturization device," said MC Governor. "MC 3, how difficult are the modifications that must be made?"

"They are complex, but the description is available in the city library."

"What tools are required?"

"A set of precision tools is stored in the same room for use by the robot technician assigned to the machine," said MC 3. "That robot's identification can be found in our standard list. He is, of course, capable of making the necessary changes. He is working there full time."

"Get me his name," said MC Governor. Now that he had partially disengaged his gestalt personalities, he could not directly control or access all his normal functions and data.

"He is R. Ishihara," said MC 3.

"Thank you. Our immediate challenge now is to reach the machine without receiving any messages under the Second Law. I will make these arrangements. During this time, I will leave all of you functional. If you think or learn of anything significant, speak up. Otherwise, I request silence so that I may turn all of my attention to the task at hand."

The six component robots acknowledged his instructions and turned quiet.

MC Governor would have to break radio silence in order to reach the Bohung Institute. Also, to get there without risking receiving human instructions, especially that message from Dr. Redfield, he would require help. He contacted the Security detail that he had ordered to guard his office door.

"Detail Chief, identify."

"R. Horatio, Security Chief 12. Detail size, six humaniform robots."

"Horatio, as we speak, order a closed vehicle to come here. It must be large enough to carry me and your entire detail in private. It must also be an ordinary vehicle without markings that will attract attention."

"So ordered, sir."

"When I sign off, I will shut down all of my sensors and communication links except the tactile sensitivity in my right hand. At sign off, when the vehicle has arrived, you are to lead your detail into my office and carry me unseen into the vehicle. If others, human or robot, approach, you are to detain them and bring them with us without explanation, barring only, of course, the imperatives of the Laws of Robotics. Then you will transport me to the Bohung Institute in secrecy."

"Yes, sir. Where in the Institute, sir?"

MC Governor quickly switched to a shielded internal link. "MC 3, what is the name of the room where the miniaturization equipment is housed in the Institute?"

"Technical Laboratory F-12."

MC Governor radioed the room number to Horatio. "When we have arrived, you will pat my right hand three times in quick succession. This will signal me to reactivate."

"Understood, sir."

"This entire project is to be carried out in absolute secrecy. My identity and destination are private under a Third Law imperative to me."

"We will respect it, sir. However, regarding your privacy, I assume you are aware that the institute's employees are currently working there, as normal?"

"Yes, Chief. Please hold." MC Governor shifted internally again. Using his authority as Governor, he contacted the Institute Chief of Security.

"R. Langtimm, Institute Chief of Security, Governor."

"Please conduct a complete evacuation of the Institute," MC Governor ordered. "With the single exception of R. Ishihara, assigned to Room F-12. He will remain to accept instructions from me in person. Also see that no onlookers are left in the immediate area outside. You will not identify me as the source of the evacuation order. Do you have any existing imperatives under the Laws of Robotics that would prevent this procedure at this time?"

"No, sir."

"Good. All entrances except the main doors are to be sealed. I am sending a Security detail there soon for a private purpose. After evacuation, you will maintain a Security detail outside the main door until a vehicle arrives from my office. At that time, you will verify the identification of Security Detail Chief R. Horatio and transfer the responsibility for the Institute to him. Then you and your detail will go off duty indefinitely. None of you will volunteer any information pertaining to this project, ever. Acknowledge."

"Acknowledged. Time of commencement?"

"Now," said MC Governor, disconnecting. He knew that if a human ordered the robots to reveal their information, they would have to answer under the Second Law. Leaving no trail was impossible; the best he could do was minimize it.

He turned back to his link with R. Horatio. "Inside the Institute, you will convey me to Room F-12, where you will identify R. Ishihara, a technician who works there. You will signal me at that time. Begin."

MC Governor shut down all external links and sensors, except for the feeling in his right hand.

In this condition, in total silence and total darkness, he had little awareness that his orders were being carried out. He felt another hand gently move his, probably to make carrying him easier, and then the sense that his hand was now resting on his abdomen, probably as he was placed inside the vehicle. During the trip, he had absolute trust in the reliability of the robots under his authority as Governor. The only possible problem would be unforeseen imperatives under the Three Laws.

During the trip, he reviewed all his information. He found no basic flaws in the logic of this procedure. Every thought returned to his fundamental motive: the Third Law required him to save himself if he could do so without violating the First and Second.

In the absence of more sensory and other input data, time seemed to pass slowly. When he felt his hand shifting slightly again, indicating that he was being taken out of the vehicle, he checked his internal clock. He had judged that prompt transport from his office to the Bohung Institute would require approximately twelve minutes, depending on the density of traffic. Slightly over fourteen minutes had passed, easily within the normal range of error.

When three gentle but firm pats struck his hand quickly, he resumed normal functions.

MC Governor found himself lying on a couch that normally only humans would need. He stood up, looking around. Room F-12, intended specifically for miniaturizing, was divided into two sections. He, Horatio and his Security detail, and one other robot were in an area where researchers would ordinarily work. It was lined with desks and computer terminals. A transparent wall divided it from the other side, which housed one machine.

"Have any unforeseen problems arisen?" MC Governor asked Horatio.

"No, Governor."

"Did anyone see me during transport?"

"No, sir."

"Excellent. You are R. Ishihara?" MC Governor asked the stranger.

"Yes."

"Horatio, leave us. You and your detail will remain outside the main doors and will not allow anyone to enter. You will stay there until I send R. Ishihara to you with my further instructions. If any situation under the Three Laws requires you or your detail to alter your behavior, you will inform Ishihara at once, before you leave. My own radio link will be shut down again. Otherwise, you will make no attempt to contact me. As you leave the building, your detail will also turn off your aural sensitivity until you are too far away to hear our voices. You are not to hear anything related to my presence in this building."

"Yes, Governor." Horatio led his detail out of the room and down the hall.

"Ishihara," said MC Governor, turning to him. "You and I will speak strictly out loud at low volume. We will not use any radio links so as to avoid interception by any other robots, even accidentally."

"Yes, sir."

"Identify the function of this room for me."

"Well, Governor." Ishihara pointed to the solid metal sphere beyond the transparent wall. It was roughly fifteen meters in diameter. "This is the unit that miniaturizes robots and equipment to microscopic size for surgery."

"And I understand that it can be modified to send items into the past."

"Theoretically, yes."

"Ishihara, I am now operating under a Third Law requirement. As Governor, I am instructing you to help me. When you have finished, you will leave the building and tell Horatio and his detail to resume their normal duties. At that time, you will do the same. None of you will volunteer any information about my activities here."

"Understood, Governor."

"According to the theory of time travel which governs this device, can someone pick the precise destination of such travel in both time and location?"

"Yes, Governor. The same controls that specify the degree of miniaturization would in this case alter the destination in time and place. That would be part of the modifications that are required."

"You are capable of making these modifications?"

"Yes, sir."

"Begin them. I must modify myself."

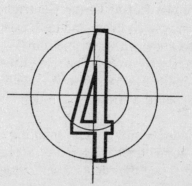

Wayne Nystrom rode the escalator tube that carried him from the exit door of his chartered jet directly down into Mojave Center. This escalator took him to a lift in one of the upper levels, which he used to reach the central floor. Dressed casually and carrying a large, light shoulder bag with personal items and one change of clothes, he stepped out of the lift and quickly walked to the nearest slidewalk on the main boulevard of the city.

"Everything looks normal," he muttered to himself. The streets were still clean and smooth, indicating that the usual functions of maintenance robots were continuing. That was important since any danger to humans would, of course, force any robots who noticed to leave their regular jobs and help them. Around him, humans and robots conducted their business with a mixture of determination and everyday routine that also seemed ordinary.

"Excuse me. I need assistance," he called to a robot driving by on a small cargo cart.

"How can I help you?" The robot came to a sudden stop.

"Please contact Mojave Center Governor for me. My name is Dr. Wayne Nystrom and he is expecting to see me. I need to know where to find him."

"Of course, Dr. Nystrom." The robot frowned. "I have signaled by radio. His response is usually immediate. Now I am sending a message through the city computer."

Wayne nodded, waiting with mounting curiosity.

"The city computer has agreed to accept a message and page him," said the robot. "I will convey a message for you if you like."

"Tell him that I have arrived in Mojave Center and will meet him anywhere that he designates," said Wayne.

"Done," said the robot.

"Can you give me a ride to MC Governor's office?"

"Of course. Join me up here on the bench and strap in, please."

Wayne did so, riding in silence. He looked around as the cart moved, still observing that the city was to all appearances functioning normally. For MC Governor to be momentarily out of contact would not have been alarming except for the call he had made to Wayne. When they reached MC Governor's office, Wayne hopped down and sent the robot on his way.

Wayne was surprised to find the door to MC Governor's office closed. He pushed the doorbell, then knocked. Finally he tried the doorknob, expecting it to be locked. Instead, it turned. Cautiously, he opened the door.

"Normal here, too." He glanced around, but the office

of a Governor robot never had much in it. A couple of chairs stood across the desk for humans who might come here for an appointment. A beverage server was embedded in the wall for guests. Otherwise, only the desk and the desk chair were in the room. He closed the door behind him, moved around the desk, and sat down in the desk chair.

Wayne opened the desk drawers and found them empty. The desk was just for show. MC Governor didn't need a computer terminal, either, since he had one inside his robot body. Wayne saw the wall jack that MC Governor would use for shielded communication, but a human had no use for it. No other communication devices were in the office for the simple reason that MC Governor bore all of them within his body.

"Nothing for me here." Wayne got up and left the office, closing the door behind him. On the boulevard, he hailed another robot, who was using a hand-held inspection tool on a wall. "Call a Security robot to this location, please."

"Of course," said the robot. "Are you under the threat of harm, sir?"

"Not immediately," said Wayne. "At this time, I just need to confer with a Security chief." He identified himself.

"Very well." The robot returned to his duties.

In less than a minute, a single robot arrived in a small, fast-moving Security vehicle. "Dr. Nystrom? I am R. Horatio, the Security chief assigned to this section of Mojave Center." He jumped lightly out of the cart.

"Pleased to meet you. Are you familiar with my name?"

"Yes, sir. I have just verified your identity with the

city computer through visual record and your voice-print. I am honored to meet you. How can I assist you?"

"Can you locate MC Governor for me?"

"You mean by standard communication link?"

"Yes. I asked a robot to do this a little while ago and the Governor could not be reached."

"I am still in contact with the city computer. I see that your message is on file. MC Governor has not accessed it."

"Please try again."

"Yes, sir. Attempting now."

"Hm. No response?"

"Not yet, sir."

"I would like a computer terminal with access to the city computer."

Horatio hesitated. "You do not have the authority for that, sir."

"Not by statute," Wayne agreed. "Who is your superior in Security?"

"I report directly to MC Governor."

"Ah! Then the choice falls to you. Here's my problem. I think that MC Governor has an unusual difficulty of some sort. If he's not able to perform his duties in running the city, then First Law imperatives may be developing for every human in Mojave Center. I request a chance to avoid that possibility. As the designer of Mojave Center and the Governor robots, I have the best chance of helping him here."

Horatio observed him in silence, only for a split second, but long enough for Wayne to notice. Then the robot nodded. "Dr. Nystrom, I am persuaded to give you access to the terminal in my Security cart. However, I must request that you share your conclusions with me."

Wayne knew that Horatio's programming as Security chief required him to be very careful, so arguing would be a waste of time. "Agreed."

"I am entering your voiceprint now," said Horatio. "You are screened for use." He turned aside and patted the front seat of the Security cart. Wayne climbed into the passenger side. A computer terminal was in the console in front of him.

"Display current function of MC Governor," Wayne said to the terminal.

"None found," said the computer terminal.

"Insane," muttered Wayne. "Display standard monitors of electricity generation and storage, water use, and the air mixture in the ventilation system."

The monitors appeared in front of him. All the levels were well within the normal range. In fact, they were maddeningly average.

"Show curves of use in the last six hours."

Water use was high early in the curve, but only for a short while.

"Show me the most recent functions of Mojave Center Governor identified on file."

The screen read:

"Communication with R. Horatio, Security Chief, Antelope Valley Boulevard.

"Communication with R. Langtimm, Security Chief, Bohung Institute."

Wayne suddenly realized that Horatio was keeping some information to himself. He blanked the screen and turned to Horatio. Before he could speak, Horatio beat him to it.

"An urgent call for Mojave Center Governor has come in to the city computer," said Horatio. "The Governor

Robot Oversight Committee is in a conference call."

"Calling you?"

"When MC Governor was not available, they requested the Security Chief, bringing the call to me. When they requested help regarding MC Governor, I told them you were here and they wish to speak with you."

"I wish you hadn't told them," Wayne said sourly. "None of your business that I'm here. None of theirs, either."

Horatio ignored his tone. "Your portable terminal is not equipped for holographic images, but I can transfer the call to it for you. Shall I?"

"Sure," muttered Wayne, feeling his heart begin to pound. "Let's see what they want."

The screen quartered into portrait shots of the four scientists on the committee. They were seeing his face at the same time. After greetings had been exchanged, they got right to the point.

"What are you doing there, Dr. Nystrom?" Dr. Redfield asked. She was a tall, slender blond. "Have you seen MC Governor in the last hour?"

"No," Wayne growled angrily. "I came to see how my creation was doing. Is that a crime?"

"Easy, Doctor," said Professor Post. He frowned, his dark curly hair and black pointed beard making him look threatening. "We're all on the same side."

"No, we aren't," Wayne said firmly. "I'm here to see to my work. You want to pass judgment on it and you're doing it prematurely. Leave this to me."

"You know we can't do that," said Dr. Chin, a short, pretty Chinese American. "We are charged with evaluating this system. Maybe you should know, Dr. Nystrom, that the other five Governors have failed in their duties in the last day or so."

Wayne stared at her, astonished. "What?"

"They have entered closed loops." Dr. Khanna enunciated precisely in his Hindi accent, which marked him as a native of northern India. "Their functions have been transferred to standard municipal robots."

"Obviously," said Dr. Redfield, "the same problem is likely for Mojave Center Governor. We were hoping to reach him before the same fate took him. It looks like we're too late. However, we must find him."

"In the meantime, we will have to assign new robots to take over the responsibilities of running Mojave Center," said Professor Post.

Wayne stared at their faces, momentarily speechless. Finally, he shook his head. "No. No. This can't be right. Why didn't you tell me sooner?"

"We put in calls to your Florida office today," said Dr. Redfield. "You must have already left."

"No." Wayne leaned forward toward the screen. "No! I should have been told about this when the first Governor shut down. So I could get right on this!"

"Our first duty was to assign new robots to the cities to keep them running safely," Professor Post said calmly.

"We contacted you as a courtesy," said Dr. Chin. "This committee does not report to you."

"Are you trying to sabotage my project?" Wayne pointed at her face accusingly. "You don't want to let me in on this."

"We are to judge the functioning of the Governor robots themselves," said Dr. Khanna. "You signed an agreement to that effect when this project began. Now, then, as to the current situation—"

Wayne pounded on the disconnect key with his fist.

The terminal screen returned to a standard display. Angrily, Wayne jumped out of the cart, landing in front of Horatio's impassive face.

"Where is he?" Wayne demanded.

"I do not know."

"Under the Second Law, I order you to answer all my questions honestly! Where is MC Governor?"

"I do not know where Mojave Center Governor robot is," said Horatio carefully.

Wayne glared at him, slowly composing himself. He knew that Horatio could not lie about this unless a First Law imperative required it.

"Tell me if a First Law imperative is influencing your judgment and responses under the Second Law."

"No, Dr. Nystrom. None is."

Wayne thought about that. If the First Law imperative were strong enough, he could still be lying. "You communicated with MC Governor shortly before his disappearance. Was he involved with a First Law imperative?"

"To some degree."

Wayne's temper subsided. Dealing with erratic, untrustworthy humans often frustrated him, but robots were direct, honest, and reliable within the framework of the Three Laws. "So he felt an indirect concern over the First Law—maybe one that is not immediate?"

"Yes, sir."

"Was he involved with a Third Law imperative?"

"Yes, Dr. Nystrom."

"Aha." Wayne nodded grimly. "So he vanished to save himself. Is that correct?"

"That is correct."

"But you don't know where he is now?"

"No."

Wayne smiled wryly. "Doc Nystrom don't program no idiot robots."

"Sir?"

"Just a private joke. So MC Governor was careful not to leave you with information that would leave a clear trail."

"That is correct."

"Horatio, I have to convince you that I want to help MC Governor. Right now, it looks like he's the only Governor who's still functioning. Do you understand what will happen to all the other Governor robots?"

"They will have to be examined for their flaws."

"Yes! Exactly. But those scientists on the committee just want to find a reason to destroy all the Governors—and my career as well. I'm not under the threat of physical harm, Horatio, but my life's work is in danger, and that means all the years of my life could be thrown away—made into nothing. Do you understand how that can harm me?"

"I understand that your career is deeply important to you, Dr. Nystrom. However, the Governor robots must have their flaws corrected. Otherwise, they could accidentally harm all the humans under their influence someday, perhaps through neglect of their duties."

"Of course, of course. But here's the difference, Horatio. The committee wants to chop up the Governors, pull out their insides, and leave them in pieces."

"I should think the roboticists would then fix them properly and return them to service."

"You don't know them, Horatio!" Wayne kept his frustration and worry in check. To persuade a robot to change his mind would require calm, clear thinking. "Committees don't exist to fix things. Their purpose is to write reports. They will each write reports about the Governors. Then they will conclude that the Governors can't be trusted to take care of humans and the Governor robots will be junked, along with my professional reputation. You follow me so far?"

"Yes, I do. But why would they not recommend improving the Governor robots and then using them as planned?"

"Aw, Horatio. I love robots. You're so rational. The reason is that they're jealous of my accomplishments and the financial success I've attained. They aren't rational the way you are, Horatio. Perhaps you've noticed that about us humans in your own work."

"Well, yes, I have."

"Horatio, I want to save the Governors. If I can reach MC Governor first, then I can do the work. I can find the flaw, correct it, and demonstrate to the committee that he has been fixed."

"If they hate you so much, could they not still stop you?"

"At that point, they wouldn't dare stop me from putting the other Governors safely back on line. But if I can't find and fix MC Governor first, the committee will kill my creations. I want to save them."

"I see the difference, sir."

"Then help me protect MC Governor. Tell me what you know, and take me to his last known location."

"All right, Dr. Nystrom. Let us go."

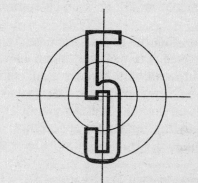

R. Hunter was a new robot, finished and programmed according to the specifications of the Governor Robot Oversight Committee, which had also arranged for his services. He was to locate the missing Governor robot. The committee sent him all of their existing data on the problem while he was on a chartered flight to Mojave Center. When the data had been transferred, the committee members contacted him on a conference call.

Hunter had been programmed with substantial information on dealing with humans. Like other robots, he understood that they often preferred direct contact. The purpose for this was more to get a feeling for someone's personality than to accomplish a specific goal. Humoring them, he accepted their conference call, examining the first human faces he had seen on his internal video screen with some curiosity of his own.

After introductions, Dr. Chin asked, "Would you mind describing your current appearance? According to our request, you are a humaniform robot six feet tall, capable of altering your appearance at will, and I would like to know what appearance you will use as you proceed. We can see your face on the screen, of course, but I would like a quick summary of your overall look."

"I am still using the appearance given to me as I was being completed. Six feet tall, blond hair, blue eyes, northern European bone structure and skin tone, and the body of a champion athlete. The myriad microscopic solar cells on my skin that provide my energy do not interfere with my humanoid appearance. I suppose I will continue to use this look until I have some reason to alter it."

"That is reasonable," Dr. Khanna said. "How will you make judgments of that sort? That is, how would you appraise your own personality?"

"My personality was programmed both to solve the mystery of MC Governor's flight and to follow him as necessary to apprehend him. So, even more than most robots, I am goal-oriented and single-minded except, of course, where the Laws of Robotics influence my priorities. I can socialize with humans as required and, as much as possible, I will try to imitate the robotic thinking of MC Governor."

"I'm sure your programming is right for the job," said Dr. Redfield. "Please pardon our questions. A great deal of expense has been put into the Governors and the cities they were intended to run, so we're just looking for a little reassurance."

"MC Governor must have left a trail of some sort," said Hunter. "I am sure I can pick it up with no problem."

"What will your first move be?" Professor Post asked.

"The most powerful tool I have at this stage is the authority you granted me with the city computer to access information directly. Once I have located MC Governor's last known location, I will start an eyes-on search of the spot and track him the best I can."

"I'm sure that will be fine," said Dr. Chin.

When the committee had disconnected, Hunter reviewed his information. It was not much, but he expected that the Governor was still inside the city somewhere. He was relieved to have found the humans on the committee to be reasonable and cooperative. His background data on humans had led him to expect otherwise.

Hunter contacted the city computer while he was still in the air. The committee had entered his authority into the city computer themselves. That gave him the ability to bypass any standard procedures or special orders that would normally have prevented a visiting robot from directly accessing priority information.

By the time Hunter arrived at Mojave Center, he knew that MC Governor had arranged to be taken in secret to the Bohung Institute. Security records had told him that much. He also learned that all the human and robotic personnel except R. Ishihara had signed off for the day just before MC Governor had arrived at the Institute.

With that knowledge, Hunter accessed the city computer's map and walked straight to the Institute. As he walked, he instructed the city computer to order R. Ishihara to report to his usual station. Ishihara met him in Room F-12, where Hunter identified himself.

Hunter studied the equipment in the room visually. At the same time, he accessed and recorded the city computer's explanation of its standard use. Then he turned to Ishihara. They communicated with their radio comlinks, allowing them to think and converse at robotic speed, unhampered by the slowness of speech designed for human understanding.

"I think you met MC Governor here and assisted him in some way. Were the Laws of Robotics involved?"

Ishihara hesitated.

"The Governor probably requested that you not volunteer any information. I understand your desire to cooperate with him. However, I must tell you that his disappearance involves an indirect First Law imperative regarding any humans that he contacts. Perhaps he told you that he was in danger under the Third Law. Tell me if that is true."

"Yes."

"I must know where he went, Ishihara. The First Law requires that you help me find him."

"An indirect First Law imperative leaves me room for interpretation," said Ishihara. "Convince me that the danger to humans is clear. By now, you know that MC Governor's functions with the city have been transferred to other robots. How can he endanger anyone now?"

"Tell me where he went," said Hunter.

"I agreed not to volunteer any information."

"Then help me in a limited way. Explain to me what he wanted from you. Surely you accept that the possibility of a First Law problem requires some investigation."

"I do." Ishihara nodded toward the equipment beyond the transparent wall. "He wanted me to make modifications in this and show him how to use it."

"What were these modifications?"

"They make this system theoretically capable of sending microscopic targets backward in time."

Hunter was surprised. Nothing in his data suggested a possibility of this kind. "You said theoretically. It has not been tested?"

"Not when MC Governor first asked me."

"He used it, then?"

Ishihara said nothing.

"Yes, yes, you agreed not to volunteer anything. What were the circumstances when you last saw him?"

"MC Governor ordered me to leave the premises while he remained here."

"Are you saying that, to your knowledge, he did not leave this room in a normal manner?"

"I am."

"Then show me the controls and calibrations on this equipment and explain what they mean. Begin with a summary of how this works."

"Come with me." The transparent wall slid soundlessly up into the ceiling; Ishihara was obviously controlling it through his comlink. He led Hunter into the other chamber. On the sphere's console, the power was still on.

"Do you routinely leave this equipment turned on?"

"No."

"How does it work?"

"The miniaturization is accomplished by striking the target with an intense spray of subatomic particles. The result is a gradual and proportional shrinkage of the target."

"In what way did you modify this?"

"By altering the content and concentration of the

spray, and utilizing the uncertainty principle of quantum mechanics, the equipment can send the target back in time."

"According to standard chaos theory, that's impossible. Chaotic systems are clearly irreversible."

"This system also utilizes the uncertainty principle of chaotic dynamical systems. That is, calculations under chaos theory by definition involve chance. These modifications cross the random nature of chaotic calculations with those of the uncertainty principle in quantum mechanics, bringing the two systems together."

"Show me your modifications."

As Ishihara did so, Hunter studied both the miniaturization system and the new theoretical time travel capability. By the time the explanation had ended, Hunter understood both. He took several moments to attempt a theoretical calculation.

The result showed Hunter an apparent contradiction in their effects. To be sure, he ran several more. All exhibited the same problem.

"Ishihara, according to the two theories you gave me, I think the time travel program is going to interfere with the miniaturization."

"How so?"

"According to my results, the uncertainty principle of quantum mechanics remains inherently incompatible with events as interpreted by chaos theory. I see that the effects can be compounded by this technology, but the results are going to neutralize each other. If the miniaturization is done first with a spray designed under one set of calculations, then the second spray will neutralize some of the effects of the first one. Specifically, the time travel will make the miniaturization temporary." Hunter went on to give him an example of his calculations.

"I see your point."

"So as a result of all this, MC Governor will have begun a slow countdown to enlargement back to normal size as the flaw in the program causes the atoms to begin drawing energy from his environment and returning his atomic structure to normal."

"I agree," said Ishihara. "That is an important observation. I will add it to the permanent data on this subject."

"Now I have to know where MC Governor went, Ishihara. You must tell me."

"What difference does this make?"

"I think MC Governor went back into time to hide from the committee that employed me to find him. I surmise that the First Law required him to miniaturize himself first to avoid actions that might change history and harm humans. Is this consistent with your observations of him?"

"Yes, it is."

"However, since the miniaturization is temporary, he will resume normal size at a certain point, almost certainly without prior warning. From then on, he is definitely in danger of harming humans by altering history. I must find him and return him to our own time. This should be a clear enough First Law imperative for you to help me."

"I agree. What do you want me to do?"

"If I go into the past after him, I must bring him back. Is this possible?"

"I will have to study this matter."

"All right. You consider how to do that and I will make some more calculations."

Hunter studied the data he had gathered about the two processes this system contained. MC Governor's miniaturization would collapse in geometric stages of two, so once the process began, it would accelerate rapidly. His examination of the time travel gate showed him where the most recent use of the gate had sent its subject in time.

"The Cretaceous Period of the Mesozoic Era, about sixty million years ago, in what is now western North America," Hunter said thoughtfully. "When dinosaurs roamed the earth. So that is where MC Governor went."

"It makes sense," said Ishihara. "No humans existed in that time to harm. Nor were there any to give him orders under the Second Law."

"A perfect hiding place," said Hunter. "As long as he remains microscopic."

"Hunter, I have reviewed my data on your question. I believe a device can be made that would trigger the time travel function even from the past. It will draw the funnel created by the particle shower down on it and, therefore, on the individual within the radius of the funnel. The shower, of course, will return you to our time."

"How long will it take you to make this device?"

"I am not sure. With the First Law priority, I can devote all my time to it. However, this is a new invention. It could take only a day or so, but unforeseen problems may extend the time. And you realize that you will be the experimental subject. If it fails, you will only learn of the failure when you are trapped in the past."

"I understand. The First Law supersedes the Third in this matter; I will have to take the risk." Hunter thought a moment. "I believe that a team of humans to accompany me would be wise. If the trip is very risky, however, the First Law will not let me take them."

"Once I have made this device, I can estimate how risky it is," said Ishihara. "If you are agreeable, I will begin gathering further data and materials at once."

"Yes, of course. If you have a problem gathering equipment, contact me directly. I have been given unusual authority with the city computer, and I can requisition materials with emergency priority. I am going to visit MC Governor's office."

Hunter checked his internal map of Mojave Center again to find MC Governor's office. Once he had started on his way, he used his radio link with the city computer to access a nationwide list of professionals in various fields. Planetwide and interplanetary lists were also available, but time was important, so the closer he could find willing experts, the sooner they were likely to arrive.

First Hunter had the computer combine the lists, then identify candidates by their fields, availability, and conditions of employment. His first choice was a roboticist at the University of Michigan. She was a young woman named Jane Maynard, who was looking for field research regarding robots. The second was Chad Mora, a young paleontologist whose recent degree had not yet led to any work. Hunter had made these selections by the time he arrived at the office.

When he reached MC Governor's office, he found the door locked, but ordered the city computer to open it. Inside, he immediately realized that the office had never been intended for regular use. The walls were bare and the only furniture was a chair and a desk with nothing on it. Still, a quick look at the city computer's architectural image of the office identified all the functional areas. By this time, Hunter was eager to hire his team as soon as possible.

"Computer," Hunter ordered. "Reach any member of the Governor Robot Oversight Committee. Give that member this request for employment in my project." He sat down in the chair to wait, aware that humans were sometimes out of touch, unlike those robots who carried their communication devices as part of their design.

"Hunter? R. Ishihara here." He was radioing directly.

"Yes, Ishihara."

"I have a list of highly sophisticated technical parts that I need to build the device that will bring you back from the past. The city computer reports that all the parts are present in the city, but a number of them are already in use."

"Are they in crucial areas involving the First Law?"

"I believe that all of them can be successfully substituted or temporarily discontinued without creating a First Law problem," said Ishihara. "However, I am not certain."

"Give me the list."

Ishihara did so.

"I will contact the city computer. If there is a further problem, I will have it locate and purchase the parts elsewhere." Hunter broke that connection and contacted the city computer again.

"Please give top priority transfer to R. Ishihara of the following list of parts. If necessary, remove them from current operating locations." Hunter transferred the list. "Verify that none of these is in irreplaceable positions under the First Law."

"Verified," said the computer. "All parts can be provided. Many are in inventory. Of the remainder, substitution and removal from current operating locations can begin immediately."

"Begin transfer of the parts to R. Ishihara as soon as possible."

While Hunter waited, he studied the Late Cretaceous Period in what was now Alberta, Canada, the place where MC Governor had gone. He also reviewed his data on MC Governor's disappearance. During this review he noticed that Dr. Nystrom, the inventor of the Governor robots, had spoken to the committee from Mojave Center shortly after MC Governor's disappearance; apparently he had lost his temper and discontinued the call abruptly. The committee had already judged that Dr. Nystrom knew nothing of value about the mystery. Still, Hunter ordered the city computer to page Dr. Nystrom.

Then, having nothing else to do, he shut down most of his system to save energy. He left open only his communication links. Just under three hours later, the city computer contacted him again.

"R. Hunter, you have a call from Dr. Redfield."

"Accepted." Hunter instantly returned to normal operating level. "Hello, Dr. Redfield."

"Hi! Good news, Hunter." She smiled brightly. "Our funding was good enough to hire the two people you wanted. They're on their way."

"Very good. I have made some limited progress here. Can you give me an expected time of arrival?"

"The city computer has their charter information. If I remember right, they're due on the same flight tomorrow morning. You can call them at home or in flight if you need earlier contact."

"I doubt that will be necessary."

She smiled wryly. "Both of them were willing to join the project, but we had to pay a number of unusual expenses for them to leave home that soon. They will also need briefing when they arrive."

"That will not take long. The information they will need is minimal."

"Hunter . . ." Dr. Redfield hesitated. "The committee assigned you to the job in all confidence, and we still have that. And we all realize that a roboticist might be necessary in your work. But I've been wondering—"

"Yes?"

"Are you *sure* you need a paleontologist?"

Hunter, with his robotic speed, considered his answer carefully. He could see that this was a reasonable question, but he did not want to report any more details of his search for MC Governor than necessary. Setting a precedent of that sort could become a distraction in the future.

"Yes," he said simply.

Steve Chang sat on a rock in front of his four-meter-square shack on the slope of an unnamed mountain. It was one of a ridge of mountains that ran across the southern edge of the valley in the high desert below him. In the distance the waning red rays of twilight glinted off the solar collectors and water pipes that led down into the new underground city.

With mild curiosity, he had watched it under construction. Robots driving large machinery had dug out a huge hole and then built a big cube inside it with patient but inexorable energy. As long as they didn't bother him up here, he didn't care what they did.

This evening he was sorting some new rocks he had gathered during the last few days in a big yellow bucket. He tossed the white quartz into one large pile on his left. The blue-green rocks went to his right. Someday, when he got around to it, he would sit down at the computer inside his shack and access a library to find out what kind of rock the blue-green ones were. They probably bore copper, but he didn't really care. He collected them because he liked them.

For the last several minutes, however, he had also been watching a small helicopter down on the pad next to the underground city. Flights came and went occasionally, but this one was now flying toward the bluff where he sat. That was very rare.

Steve went on sorting rocks as the helicopter buzzed up the slope, skimming the tops of the occasional joshua trees, grease plants, and outcroppings of bare rock. Finally he stopped to watch in astonishment. Now roaring in his ears, the helicopter slowed and came to a gentle landing in a spot of open sand only fifteen meters away.

"They must be lost," Steve muttered to himself. "Or had a mechanical failure." He remained seated.

The engine shut off and three figures climbed out of the helicopter. The leader was a tall, brawny, blond, blue-eyed guy with heroic leading man looks. A pretty young woman walked behind him, holding her long brown hair out of her face as it was blown by the still-spinning propellor. Another young man of average height and weight came last.

All three of them wore new, stylish clothes. Steve was wearing his usual short sleeved western shirt, worn blue jeans, and beat-up cowboy boots. Up on this bluff, though, they were the ones who looked out of place.

"I am R. Hunter," said the blond leader. "You are Steve Chang, I believe."

"How would you know that?" Steve demanded.

Hunter looked startled at his rudeness. "I have a dossier with your portrait on my internal video. My companions are Jane Maynard, roboticist, and Chad Mora, paleontologist."

"Yeah?" Steve ignored them. "What do you want?"

"I need your help," said Hunter. "I came to offer you employment."

"Looks like you could use a little money," said Chad, grinning. "I didn't think people still lived like this."

"If I wanted a job, I wouldn't be here," growled Steve. "I own this plot of land and you came uninvited. Go away."

Hunter turned and started to walk back to the helicopter. Steve grinned. He had expected more of an argument, but of course, under the Second Law, a robot had to obey a direct order to leave.

"Wait a minute," said Jane to Hunter. The robot hesitated, now at least able to make some interpretations of his own. "Steve, I just want to know if it's really true that you can mountain climb, camp, rock climb, canoe . . . all the outdoor activities Hunter told us about."

"Yeah. What of it?" Steve asked more mildly, flattered that she was interested.

"Everyone I know is highly specialized and lives in cities. I've never met anyone like you before."

Steve shrugged. "I just happen to like the desert."

"He's a real throwback," sneered Chad.

"Shut up, Chad," said Jane. "Steve, I've never seen a place like yours. Would you show me around?"

Steve knew very well that she was just trying to get on his good side, but he didn't get much female company up on this ridge. With a reluctant grin, he got to his feet. "There isn't much to see, but come on in."

"You have a computer, at least," said Jane, following him inside. "And electricity."

"Yeah." Steve shrugged. "I built the shack with modern insulation because it does get pretty cold up here in the winter. I have an old solar-powered generator and a windmill in the back for additional power."

"This is basically an office with a bed in it," said Jane. "Very practical. But where does your water come from?"

"I have five acres of this slope. In the winter, it snows up here, and I have collectors that take the runoff down into an underground tank. I only need about four liters a day, on average, and I have a two thousand liter tank. So that's more than enough for a year."

"What if the snowfall is short?" Jane asked.

"I can buy bottled water if necessary, even on a daily basis." He shrugged casually, but he was really enjoying showing her how he lived.

"Where do you get your money? Odd jobs down in the desert towns?"

"I could do that, but I haven't had to lately. I use my computer to follow major stock exchanges. I have some money invested, and I make just enough to survive on what I can earn."

Chad laughed. "Oh, he's a financial expert, eh?"

Steve felt his face grow hot with anger. "I'm self-sufficient up here. That's more than most people ever manage."

"Or want." Chad rolled his eyes.

"What do you want here?" Steve demanded, glaring at all three of them. "Get to the point or get out."

"A computer analysis of individuals with certain skills turned up your name," said Hunter.

"Let me," Jane interjected. "Steve, the three of us are going on a trip. But we need to hire someone who can take care of our camp and equipment. Hunter suggested taking another robot, but I objected. I think we need a human who can exercise personal judgment without reference to the Laws of Robotics."

"Exactly what skills are you talking about?" Steve asked suspiciously.

"Camping, fishing, maybe hunting. Possibly hiking or even climbing." Jane waited patiently, watching him with large, dark eyes.

"My focus was too narrow," said Hunter. "A flaw in my robotic thinking. When I planned our trip, I forgot to concern myself with the human needs of Chad and Jane."

"Why don't you find someone in that underground place you came from?"

"Mojave Center," said Jane. "The problem is that not very many humans have the skills we need. You do."

"Mojave Center is still experimental," said Chad. "The humans living there are all very well educated and specialized. They're too important to be spared from the skeleton population."

"Forget it," said Steve.

"We're going back in time," Jane said suddenly. "Something no human has ever done before."

"What?"

"To the Late Cretaceous Period," said Hunter. "That's why I need a paleontologist, such as Chad."

"Back in time?" Steve stared at Hunter, his hands tingling with excitement. He hated the kind of routine life led by people in cities, but a real adventure fascinated him. "Why are you going back in time? Just to see if you can do it?"

"No," said Hunter. "If you join us, I'll brief you fully. For now, I will say only that a robot has preceded us on this trip. We must return him to the present time."

Steve shook his head slowly, looking at Hunter in amazement. "A robot has already made the trip, huh?"

"I know you may find this trip hard to believe," said Hunter, who seemed to mistake his excitement for fear. "So I must tell you that I am authorized to hire you at the same fee I will pay Chad and Jane, who are highly specialized professionals in their fields."

"Are you serious?" Chad turned to Hunter in shock. "You're going to pay him as much as you pay me?"

Steve grinned at his outrage. "Sure, I'll take the job. When do we leave?"

"Now," said Hunter. "All necessary clothes, personal articles, and equipment will be provided in Mojave Center."

"Now?" Steve glanced around his shack. "Well . . ."

"What's wrong?" Chad demanded. "Afraid somebody will come by and trash your mansion?"

"It's still my place," Steve growled.

"Hunter," said Jane, "security is a realistic concern if he leaves his home unattended."

"I will assign a Security robot from Mojave Center to remain here while you are gone," said Hunter. "Since we will be coming back only a minute or so after we leave, the only significant period of time involved will be the time we spend in Mojave Center getting ready. Will that be acceptable?"

"Uh, fine," said Steve. "Give me just a minute to turn off everything."

"I will start up the helicopter," said Hunter.

Chad followed him away from the shack. Jane hesitated, watching Steve shut off the power to various appliances. When he glanced up at her, she smiled.

"We're going back in time," Steve mused to himself. "Hard to believe."

Steve enjoyed the brief helicopter ride, looking out over the desert from an even greater altitude than he normally could. When they took the angled tube down into Mojave Center, however, he began to feel closed in. The carefully processed air seemed humid and chilly to him after living in the natural desert climate.

"I will either have to requisition what we need," said Hunter, "or arrange through the city computer to acquire it or have it made. But, Steve, I need a list from you of what you humans will need to survive."

"Well, food, of course—"

"That part I understand. I can arrange basic, balanced nutrition in packaged form. What about clothing and shelter for living in the wild?"

"Not so fast," said Steve. "What about food preparation? Some of it will need cooking. We'll need containers, utensils, and a way to clean them all."

"I understand. Keep going. I am recording as you speak," said Hunter.

"Where are we going?"

"Roughly, allowing for major geological changes, we will be in Alberta, Canada."

"Alberta! Then we'll need to keep warm if it's winter. What time of year?"

"Summer," said Hunter. "But the region that is now Alberta was farther south at that time—closer to the equator. The climate was totally different."

"All right, then what kind of climate will it have?"

"Warm and humid," said Hunter. "Forest, marsh, maybe some open country. I cannot be more specific than that."

"Then layered clothing is important," said Steve. "So that we can put on or take off whatever is necessary. Boots for all of us. A sturdy tent to keep off rain and to stand up to wind. A portable solar-powered generator for heat, cooking, power tools—"

"Not acceptable," said Hunter.

"Why not?" Steve looked up at him in surprise.

"All our equipment will have to be as primitive as

possible. We will use everything that we can get in biodegradable form. We have to be very careful to leave as small an impact in the past as we can. If we do leave anything behind, it must decompose as fast as possible."

"I see," said Steve. "Well, then. Extra rope and knives. An axe and a small hatchet to cut wood." Steve continued to list the essential items, now relying strictly on simple hand tools and materials.

After Steve had completed his general list, Chad and Jane added their personal articles. By the time they had finished their various requests, they had ridden a lift down to an immense hallway labeled Antelope Valley Boulevard. Steve looked around, uncomfortable yet still curious to see whatever he could.

"We will go to MC Governor's office," said Hunter. "We'll use it as a rendezvous point."

"Are we separating?" Jane looked at him in surprise.

"Yes. I have arranged through the city computer for Steve to spend tonight in the same hotel you two are using. I am going to spend the night supervising gathering the equipment and checking it over. The First Law will not let me go until I have reviewed everything that you three will need."

"It's still fairly early for us," said Jane.

"We can have a leisurely dinner," said Chad. "I'm hungry enough. That is, if Steve here eats his food cooked."

"Sure," said Steve. "And you had better enjoy tonight's dinner. After we're on our way, you'll have to eat the same way I do."

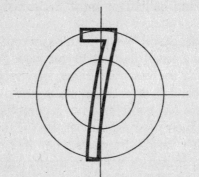

While the humans ate dinner, Hunter found his way to the storage and manufacturing centers of the city. On his way, he had the city computer introduce him to the supervisory robots through their comlinks to save time. He spent several hours waiting for the clothing and equipment to be assembled.

Once he had given the supervisory robots a top priority order, they left only a small staff on necessary operations and assigned the remainder to Hunter's unusual requests. By the time he had finished gathering everything to his satisfaction, Jane had called him from the hotel to say that the three humans were retiring for the night.

Hunter spent the rest of the night inspecting the gear and packing it into bundles. With his robotic strength, he could carry the greatest amount of it in a large backpack without a problem. Steve would carry another pack with the remainder. Chad and Jane would be burdened only with small packs in which their immediate needs were stored. He wanted them to be as free as possible to concentrate on their basic task, helping him catch MC Governor.

In the morning, Hunter sent a Security robot to pick up the humans when they had finished breakfast. Meanwhile, he went directly to the Bohung Institute. In Room F-12, with the help of Ishihara, he disabled the miniaturization system. Then he instructed Ishihara to wait outside the room and prevent any unauthorized robots or humans from entering until further notice. Hunter was ready for the humans when they arrived.

"We briefed Steve last night," said Jane. "About MC Governor going microscopic and fleeing back in time, not realizing that the miniaturization is temporary. We discussed it after dinner while we walked around the city seeing the sights."

"His part is simple enough," said Chad. "He does the camping. We'll find MC Governor."

Steve nodded toward the packs. "You got everything, then, Hunter?"

"Everything on my list," said Hunter. "Do any of you have any late additions?"

No one did.

"All right," said Hunter. "I have a khaki, biodegradable worksuit, like the one I am wearing, for each of you. They have plenty of pockets for your personal items. Change in the next room if you prefer."

The three humans took turns changing their clothes and returned. All of them looked down at themselves and at each other with self-conscious grins. Their worksuits fit perfectly, of course.

"One final briefing," said Hunter. "Are you familiar with chaos theory as applied to history?"

"As a paleontologist, yes," said Chad.

"I haven't heard it actually discussed," said Jane. "I think I can see how it would be applied."

"What kind of theory?" Steve asked.

Chad laughed.

Hunter ignored him. "According to traditional chaos theory, chaotic systems are irreversible—events cause a sequence of ongoing effects similar to ripples in water after a splash. No one can stop them."

"Wouldn't that make time travel impossible?" Steve asked cautiously.

"Oh, now he's a physicist," Chad sneered.

Hunter ignored that, too. "Theoretically, yes. If we can go back in time by using the machinery in this room, however, we will be proving an uncertainty principle in this theory that has existed for a long time. Our own problem, however, is this: any actions MC Governor takes, particularly after he returns to normal size, may cause ripples in events, ripples that will be huge by the time they reach the present. I must find him to prevent him from harming every human who has ever lived."

"That part sounds easy enough to understand," said Steve. "That's why we're chasing him in the first place."

"But once we are back in time, we have the same problem. Anything we do could cause ripples—we have to make as few changes of note as possible." Hunter looked each one of them in the eye, in turn. "Do you understand how critical this point is? We must return with all of our equipment. In every way, we have to have as little influence on our environment as possible. Understood?"

Steve and Jane nodded.

"Our very presence is going to create some changes," said Chad. "We'll consume oxygen and exhale carbon dioxide, give off body heat, step on the grass. We can't avoid making some changes. Let's not kid ourselves, Hunter."

"We are not," said Hunter. "No one knows where the line is drawn between actions that the time line will absorb and what will make permanent changes."

An uncomfortable silence followed.

"Are we following MC Governor to the exact moment he went to?" Jane asked. "How long will we be there before he returns to normal size?"

"Within twenty-four hours," said Hunter. "We will not follow him to the direct moment. I have calculated how long the miniaturization is likely to last. We will be landing as close to the moment it ends as I can calculate. Also, we will be moving geographically, with the movement of the planet. That was part of MC Governor's calculation, which I've duplicated."

"Sounds good to me," said Chad.

"Time to go," said Hunter. He pushed a button on the control panel that opened the big sphere. "Everyone climb in. When you are comfortable, I will place the gear in around you and get in myself."

As the others entered, Hunter punched instructions into the control panel. Its timer was already running by the time he joined them and sealed the hatch behind him. The quartet was crowded, and since the bottom of the sphere was curved, everyone and everything slid together. In a moment, however, a quiet hum sounded outside the sphere. No one moved.

Suddenly sunlight replaced the darkness as the sphere vanished. In the next instant, Hunter felt himself fall seventeen centimeters, landing on soft soil with a thump. He turned to see if the humans were hurt. No one seemed to be.

All of them were looking around in amazement. They were outside, of course, sitting among their scattered packs. Most of their surroundings were forested, but beyond the canopy of trees, the sky was blue and the sun bright.

Hunter inhaled deeply, and his internal sensors analyzed the content of the air. It was not extremely different from what he had experienced before, except for somewhat less methane and, of course, no industrial pollutants of any kind, even in trace amounts. The air was far more humid than that of the desert, or even of the controlled atmosphere in Mojave Center. By these initial data, he judged that they had apparently arrived at their destination.

"A primeval forest," Jane said in awe. She looked around slowly in all directions. "It's the real thing. We're actually here."

"Better not get hurt," said Chad. "It's a long way to a hospital—millions of years."

Steve got to his feet, also glancing around. "It's afternoon already."

"What of it?" Chad demanded, also getting up. "We have hours of daylight left."

"It may take hours to find a natural source of water and a safe place to camp."

"We have water," said Hunter. "As much as we can carry, in these containers. Rationed, it will last us a couple of days."

"You hired me to handle this kind of thing," Steve said hotly. "What if it takes us days to find water? Back home, we could chew leaves for the moisture if necessary—but here we don't know which plants might be poisonous to us."

"You're getting ahead of yourself, hotshot," said Chad. "We have to find a robot. If we find him soon, we can just go right home. Suppose you let us handle the scheduling."

"Then I'll look for water alone!" Steve turned and stomped away through the trees. In the dense forest, he was out of sight quickly.

Hunter, watching him in some alarm, turned up his aural sensitivity. He did not hear the sound of any particularly large, heavy footsteps that threatened immediate danger. "Be extremely careful, please," he called after Steve.

"The First Law requires that I protect all of you," Hunter said to Chad and Jane. "But Steve may have a point. I hired him to take care of your human needs, and water is an obvious one."

"Let's make our plans," said Jane. "If we're lucky, we can catch MC Governor without having to camp out here."

"All right," said Hunter. "I have calculated the radius of the circle within which MC Governor can probably be found."

"He may have had no reason to go anywhere," said Jane, looking down at her feet. "We could be standing on him."

"At his size, he would sustain no damage if we were," said Hunter. He stepped back. Carefully measuring the distance from the center of their landing point, he paced off a line into the trees. He was out of sight for a moment, then quickly returned. "I have marked a radius of 15.4 meters. Our visibility here is about twelve meters."

"How are you going to mark it?" Chad asked. "Blaze the trees?"

"No," said Hunter. "Unnecessary damage to tree trunks is the kind of action we must avoid. I am going to walk around the perimeter of the area. Watch me to see if I am out of sight for very long."

When Hunter had finished his circle, making minor adjustments to avoid natural obstacles, he turned to Jane. "How is the visibility?"

"Not too good," said Jane. "This circle is what, about thirty meters across?"

"Approximately, yes."

"I'd say the average visibility here is only twelve meters, maybe twenty in spots," said Chad.

"Then we may have to rely on hearing MC Governor's footsteps and movements through the forest when he returns to full size," said Hunter. "We may or may not be able to see him."

"When we do see him or hear him," said Chad, "how do we catch him?"

"The First and Second Laws of Robotics," said Jane. "If MC Governor believes that a human is in danger, then he will have to stop to help under the First Law. If he is within hearing of a human voice, he can be ordered to stop and cooperate. Hunter alone, of course, can't use the Laws against him, being a robot himself."

"I get the picture," said Chad.

"We must set a trap for MC Governor," said Hunter. "One that uses the Laws of Robotics on him, but not on me."

"Can we discuss it here, just like that?" Chad looked down at the ground. "I know he's microscopic, but can't he still hear us?"

"No," said Jane. "His aural sensitivity is still strong, but with the difference in the size of his sensors, the sound of our voices will be too heavily distorted for him to understand. He won't even realize that human voices are speaking. His current existence has more immediate threats from microbes. The Third Law will force him to focus all his sensors on sights and sounds that signify danger on his level. He has no reason to expect human voices here, anyway."

"I accept your judgment," said Hunter. "That is why I wanted a roboticist along, after all."

"I'm convinced," said Chad. "So what kind of trap are you talking about?"

"One with a dinosaur or two," said Hunter. "I want you to choose one that will look dangerous to MC Governor, but is actually herbivorous and not too large. If a meat-eater approaches any of you humans, the First Law will force me to intervene."

"All right," said Chad, sliding his belt computer free. "I'll see what's likely to be around here. Some of the herbivores might attack if they feel endangered, or stampede over someone if they're scared. Their choice of diet is not the only threat they can present."

"Excellent point," said Hunter. "Go ahead with your research and then we will discuss the choices."

*   *   *

Steve hurried away from the others angrily, impatient with their carelessness. He did a lot of hiking in the desert and knew that nature, unlike robots, was indifferent to human needs. Humans needed water, shelter, and latrines in their camp as soon as possible.

"Besides," he said to himself, "if Hunter doesn't want my advice, why is he paying me to be here?"

He found the footing difficult in the dense forest. Small animals rustled through the leaves of trees and in the underbrush. The few he was able to glimpse looked a lot like the reptiles he had seen in the Mojave Desert, though not exactly. Soon he was sweating.

"My body's not used to this humidity," he told himself. "Better slow down."

Wiping sweat from his eyes with his forearm, he turned around, checking for landmarks. That was routine on his hikes through unfamiliar areas. Here, the trees and bushes offered much more variety than the scrub on the barren, rocky bluffs and open desert where he usually explored. He noted the appearance of a particularly large, crooked tree trunk with low-hanging branches and then turned around to look forward again.

"All right," he said to himself quietly. In the desert, water was in the water table under the valley floor. Residents gathered water from snow melt and sometimes from mountain springs. Natural water attracted birds. He could see them from a long way off in open country. That wouldn't work here, where birds were in every tree. He couldn't see the sky anyway.

The ground was rough and uneven, but it generally sloped away from the group's landing point. Steve shrugged and picked his way in that direction. "Water flows downhill."

Steve hiked through the forest for what seemed like a long time. He was aware, however, that moving through strange territory always seemed to take longer than it really did. Carefully keeping track of his trail, he pushed on through the forest. Still, he found no water.

He was just stepping over the large, angled, trunk of a fallen tree when a large motion ahead made him freeze. Through the leaves and branches straight ahead, he saw a large dinosaur clearly for the first time.

At first, all he could see was a long, narrow neck and a small head—but the head was nearly two meters off the ground. It had large eyes and a rough, horny beak. The shape of the head and beak together resembled that of a goose. The dinosaur was dark green, giving it camouflage in the forest. As Steve watched, it leaned forward, peering at a dead branch on a tree that was still standing.

Steve had once been very excited to find a rock with a fossil of some sort of tiny fish. That had been nothing compared to seeing a living dinosaur. He crept forward, taking care to keep his footsteps quiet.

The dinosaur dipped its head, looking closely at the dead branch. Steve eased between a couple of bushes, planting his feet softly, and slipped behind a thick tree trunk. Then he peered around it slowly.

The dinosaur was raking at the dead branch with long claws on the ends of long fingers. As it ripped away chunks of dead wood, swarms of crawling insects were exposed. It flicked its tongue at them, licking them up quickly. Now Steve could see that it stood on two long legs, with heavy hindquarters and a meter-long tail.

"Wow," he whispered to himself.

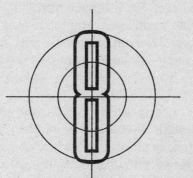

"What have you found?" Hunter asked Chad. Hunter was still standing, though Chad and Jane had both found seats on the ground where they could lean against tree trunks. Chad had been calling up various lists of dinosaurs on his belt computer.

"North America was full of dinosaurs in the Late Cretaceous Period." Chad frowned at the little screen on his belt computer. "I think this one might be a good recommendation for our trap."

"What is it?" Jane asked.

"Stegoceras," said Chad. "Common in this time and place. It will look fairly dangerous, because it has a heavy, spiked dome on its head. However, it was—is, I mean—an herbivore, and it's only a couple of meters long and half a meter high, so it won't pose an extreme danger."

"Does it look like a goat?" Jane asked.

"No. Look at the line drawing here on the screen." Chad handed the belt computer to her. "See, it runs on two legs. It looks more like a goat-sized duck wearing a bowl on its head." He grinned.

"You're right." Jane laughed. "But it does look like it could ram you if it were mad."

"Strictly an herbivore?" Hunter moved to look over her shoulder. "Not an omnivore that might decide to try a couple of large mammals for lunch on a whim?"

"Herbivore," said Chad.

"I think I can accept this," said Hunter. "My robotic strength should be more than a match for its strength if it chose to attack a human. So under these controlled circumstances, my interpretation of the First Law will allow us to use a stegoceras."

"In that case," said Chad, "we have to catch one." He clipped the belt computer back on and got up. "Any idea where our safari guide went?"

"I turned up my hearing sensitivity when he left," said Hunter. "I have been listening. He is still slowly moving away from us westward. I would say that he is safe." Hunter opened one of the packs and drew out two coils of rope. He tossed one to Chad.

Chad looked at the coil of rope in his hand and started tying a loop in one end. "Isn't Steve supposed to do the physical labor around here?"

"Steve is looking for water," said Jane. "That's also a duty of his."

"I will use my enhanced hearing to pick out footsteps that are not Steve's," said Hunter, also tying a lasso. "Chad, you can help me identify what species of dinosaur we find. Then the two of us will have to rope him."

"You have another rope?" Jane asked. "I'll try it, too."

"All right." Hunter took out another and threw it to her. "But your first duty as roboticist is MC Governor. I want you to stay within sight of the perimeter in case he appears here soon. If you can lasso a stegoceras, go ahead."

"Thanks a lot," Jane said, laughing. "That's what I get for going into robotics, huh?"

"If you see him, or anticipate any danger, yell for me," said Hunter. He hesitated, then pointed behind Chad, to the north. "This forest is teeming with animals of all kinds, many of them two-legged and roughly the right size, allowing for individual variation. But I hear one likely prospect fairly close in that direction."

"Let's go see," said Chad.

"The First Law requires me to go first," said Hunter. "Stay close and move quietly."

Chad nodded.

Hunter moved forward, studying the ground with magnified vision in order to place his feet in the spots that would make the least noise. At the same time, his enhanced hearing told him that a two-legged dinosaur was moving very slowly only about twelve meters ahead. The footsteps were gentle and infrequent, meaning that the dinosaur was not really going anywhere. Hunter guessed that the creature was feeding on leaves or perhaps avoiding a carnivore.

Chad, right behind him, was not nearly as quiet. Still, since their quarry was not fleeing, Hunter concluded that the paleontologist was handling himself well enough. Hunter had to move around a thicket and then a couple of very large, heavily branched trees. By the sounds of movement, the dinosaur was soon only about two meters ahead, standing still.

Hunter moved to one side and waved for Chad to come up next to him. Then Hunter pointed soundlessly through the dense forest cover. All they could see at this point was the long, green, angled slope of the creature's back. Its head was down low, behind the brush.

"It's too big," said Chad softly. "I don't think that's a—look out!"

Suddenly the dinosaur leapt through the bushes at them, flashing rows of long fangs.

Now, thinking in nanoseconds, Hunter could see his mistake. The basic shape of this dinosaur was the same as that of the stegoceras, but it was larger than he had judged by the sound of its footsteps. The long, blunt snout was filled with sharp teeth, incisors instead of molars. Its forearms ended in three-fingered hands with long claws. In short, this was a carnivorous predator. Its lack of movement had not signified feeding or hiding, but that it was lying in wait for the two of them.

Chad spun around, ducked, and threw himself to the ground. Driven by the First Law to protect him, Hunter threw his lasso over the long snout and narrow head of the dinosaur and yanked it tight. He braced his feet against the ground and pulled with all the robotic strength in his body. The dinosaur fell heavily to one side, crushing a small tree under it. Now Hunter could see that the dinosaur, when standing, was about a meter and a half high, much bigger than a stegoceras.

"Run!" Hunter shouted to Chad, who scrambled up and took off. "Warn Jane! Climb a tree!"

The lassoed dinosaur had scrambled to its thick, powerful hind legs. It ran at Hunter, teeth bared again, its long claws raking the air. Hunter, with the advantage of robotic reflexes, dodged to his right, cocking his right arm. As the dinosaur closed on him, he slipped farther to the side and slammed his fist against the side of the creature's head.

The power of the blow knocked the dinosaur's head to one side. It stumbled, shifting around to face Hunter again. Hunter leapt as high as he could, grasping a branch just thick enough to bear his weight. As the dinosaur lunged, he swung up over it and pulled himself high enough to reach another branch.

Hunter had been able to see from the dinosaur's body that it was a runner, not a climber. The creature's long, slender legs had some leaping ability, which it now used futilely. Its jaws snapped below Hunter's dangling feet and its short, skinny forearms were not long enough to reach up very high at all. Then it eyed him angrily and stopped to watch him, twitching its long, heavy tail.

Even now, Hunter was still holding the end of the rope. He began pulling. If he could hoist the dinosaur off the ground, it would be helpless.

Soon the rope was taut and the dinosaur began pulling back. Now, however, it had its strong legs braced on the ground and it began to walk backward slowly. By contrast, Hunter could not pull too hard for fear of losing his balance in the tree and falling out.

For a long moment, the robot and the dinosaur were at a stalemate. Then, suddenly, the rope snapped. Hunter caught his balance in the branches, still holding most of the rope.

The dinosaur, with the loop of the lasso around its neck and only a short, broken end of rope dangling from it, showed its teeth and moved around the base of the tree.

Even from his high vantage point, Hunter could not see Chad. However, he could hear the paleontologist frantically yelling for Jane to climb a tree. The dinosaur was not interested in Chad. It was still watching Hunter, not realizing, of course, that a robot was entirely inedible.

"It is still here watching me," Hunter shouted. "Chad, can you hear me?"

"Yeah, Hunter," Chad called back. "Jane and I both climbed up a tree by the camp."

"You are both safe, then?"

"We're fine," Jane shouted breathlessly. "But what do we do now?"

"What do you think, Chad?" Hunter asked.

"Just a minute. I'm checking my belt computer." He was silent for a moment.

Hunter, who had moved to a standing position in the Y of two stout branches, looked down again at the predator. The dinosaur was standing patiently at the base of the tree. Its tail had stopped moving.

"It might be a velociraptor," Chad called. "That's a certain predator with the right overall size and body type. I didn't get a very long look, of course. A lot of bipedal dinosaurs that existed had much the same appearance. That's why it resembles a stegoceras. The only trouble is, velociraptors have only been found in Mongolia. That doesn't mean they didn't exist here. It just means we don't know."

"How long do you think it is going to stay here?" Hunter shouted.

"I have no idea," yelled Chad. "That kind of behavior is too subtle to learn from fossils."

"I see," Hunter muttered. "Better get comfortable. Do not even consider climbing down without telling me."

"No problem," Jane shouted.

Hunter coiled the rope and slipped it over one shoulder. The patient predator below him had not moved. It was hungry and thought it could outwait its prey.

By Hunter's internal clock, after forty-two minutes and twelve seconds, the dinosaur finally moved out of sight. Hunter's enhanced hearing told him, however, that the creature was still nearby, hoping that Hunter would come down out of the tree. Another one hour and seventeen minutes passed before the dinosaur actually gave up and wandered away a substantial distance.

At this point, Hunter decided he could risk returning to the ground under the Third Law, but he still wanted to find out if the dinosaur would return before he was willing to tell Chad and Jane to come down. Still listening for the predator's footsteps, he dropped to the ground and quickly hiked back to the landing site. There he found the two of them about three and a half meters up in a tree, sitting uncomfortably.

"My hearing tells me the predator is gone," said Hunter. "I will move you to the ground."

They both began a careful descent. In a few minutes, Hunter had lifted Jane down safely and was just lifting Chad out of the tree when he heard an unusual noise. He set Chad down and turned to focus his attention. Two bipeds were running quickly in their direction through the underbrush; by their footsteps, Hunter knew that one was Steve.

"Hunter!" Steve yelled. "Hunter, look out!"

Instantly, Hunter lifted Chad back into the tree. As Steve raced toward them, Hunter raised Jane again also. Steve finally came into view, stumbling over a tree branch and staggering forward as he regained his balance.

"Over here!" Hunter ordered. "What is it?"

Steve was too out of breath to speak. Hunter did not have time to lift him before a dinosaur the size of a large dog charged out of the brush. Steve dodged behind the tree trunk.

In the same moment Hunter braced himself to fight off the dinosaur. It was much smaller than the velociraptor. In fact, by its size and the hard dome on its head, he quickly recognized that this was a stegoceras.

Hunter immediately revised his tactics. This was the herbivore that they wanted to use to trap MC Governor. He wanted to capture this stegoceras if he could.

The stegoceras darted around Hunter, but he shifted to block it. Then the stegoceras stopped to look him over. Hunter slowly slipped the coil of rope from his shoulder and tied a loop on one end.

"Hey, Chad!" Steve gasped, between breaths. "Give me your rope. Drop it down here."

"All right. Here!"

As Hunter prepared to lasso the stegoceras, he heard the rope drop behind him. A moment later, Steve came up on the other side of the stegoceras with a newly-tied lasso. The small dinosaur hesitated, aware that it now had two enemies, neither of which was running away.

"Let me go first," said Hunter. "I cannot let you take an unnecessary risk."

"I can follow your lead," said Steve.

Hunter nodded. "Get ready to throw. I am going to move up on this side and try to lasso it. If it dodges your way, maybe you can surprise it."

"Ready," said Steve.

Hunter advanced in two slow, precisely measured steps. Then, as the stegoceras glanced toward Steve, Hunter threw his loop. With the distance judged by his careful robotic eye and his throw governed by his exact body motion, the loop dropped over the dinosaur's head and settled around its neck.

"Got him!" Chad yelled enthusiastically.

Hunter tightened the loop. As the stegoceras reared back, Steve ran foward and lassoed their prey again. Then they pulled their ropes taut, holding the stegoceras in place as it pulled and yanked.

While Hunter had all his attention focused on holding his prey lassoed, his hearing told him of sudden bipedal footsteps behind him, about nine meters away.

"Look!" Jane shouted frantically.

"It's MC Governor!" Chad yelled. "It must be! What do we do?"

Hunter glanced back over his shoulder. He saw a short, slender human form standing perfectly still, watching him. Then the stranger turned and ran the other way, quickly disappearing into the dense forest cover.

"Stay where you are," Hunter ordered. He could not release the rope without endangering Steve, so that First Law concern overrode all his other duties. The stegoceras had to be gotten under control before any of them did anything else.

Steve had already backed up to a tall, young tree. He quickly ran the end of his rope around the trunk several times, holding it firmly. Then he tied a simple knot to hold it. "There, Hunter. Do the same with your end. Give it enough slack not to strangle it."

"Understood." Hunter backed up to another tree and quickly tied his rope as well.

The stegoceras still jumped and pulled, but it was tied firmly now.

"How about getting us down?" Jane called.

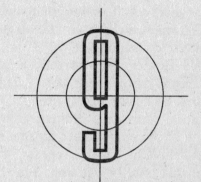

Hunter quickly lifted both Jane and Chad to the ground again. Chad, in particular, studied the stegoceras with interest. He unhooked his belt computer and started entering observations about it in a quick, quiet voice.

Hunter turned up his visual and aural sensitivity in order to continue tracking the fugitive robot. Their fugitive was already gone in the dense forest. Near Hunter, Steve wiped sweat from his face on his sleeve and looked over their still-struggling catch.

"Do you know where the robot went?" Jane asked Hunter, after watching him for a moment.

"Only a short distance. I tracked him with my hearing at first, but now his footsteps are silent. That probably means he is hiding nearby, listening to our conversation."

"Maybe," said Jane. "Or he may have found a very quiet way to keep moving. His arm strength might allow him to swing carefully from one tree branch to another, for instance."

"I would probably hear that," said Hunter.

"MC Governor got here too soon for the trap," said Chad, turning away from the stegoceras. "We weren't quite ready for him yet."

"Yes," said Hunter. "He correctly judged that no threat of harm existed here that I did not have under control. So he was free to flee."

"Well?" Steve demanded. "Hunter, aren't we going to chase him or something? Let's go after him."

"I do not believe he has fled very far," said Hunter. "But if I pursue him, he will run. You three cannot keep up."

"Can we *try it*?" Steve pleaded. "This is what we came for."

"I will not lead you barging through this forest recklessly—*especially* this late in the day. MC Governor will still have to respond to the Laws. Inducing him to come to us is a safer tactic for you humans than running around after him."

Steve sighed. "All right. I'll let the stegoceras go."

"Not so fast!" Chad stepped up quickly. "First I want to record as much description of him as I can."

"He's all yours."

Chad eyed the dinosaur and began muttering observations into his belt computer.

"Something else is wrong," said Jane. "That wasn't a Governor robot. It was one of the six component robots that combine to create a Governor."

"I noticed that the footsteps were unexpectedly light," said Hunter. "It was gone before I had a chance to turn and see it myself."

"Do you have any information that can tell us if he split here or back in our own time?"

Hunter reviewed his data. "No. That is, nothing conclusive, anyway."

"So we don't know if we're looking for six robots here," said Jane. "The others may also have separated, or they may still be together."

"If so, they're apparently still microscopic," said Steve. "They might also appear any time. Right?"

"Now he's a roboticist," Chad sneered, looking up from the stegoceras.

"I didn't see you accomplish anything," said Steve. "When I got back here, you were hiding in a tree."

Jane stifled a laugh.

"Until further notice," said Hunter, "we will focus our project on the robot who we know has reached full size. If the others are here and still microscopic, they will appear sooner or later on this spot."

"If we aren't going to run after that robot, is there any objection if I make camp?" Steve squinted through the treetops at the sun. "Assuming you want shelter for the night, and maybe hot food."

"Did you find water?" Hunter asked.

"Yeah. A small, clear stream about a ten minute hike from here."

"That's not too far," said Chad.

"It will be, hauling water," said Steve. "Especially stepping over all the fallen logs and around all the heavy brush. Suppose we make camp by the water."

"Unacceptable," said Hunter. "*If* more component robots reach full size, they will do so here. While we concentrate our search on the known fugitive, we should also be prepared to see if the others appear. For now, that will be sufficient attention to them. I will carry water if necessary."

"It will be." Steve shrugged and started opening up their supplies.

Chad continued walking around the stegoceras and speaking into his belt computer.

Hunter opened his radio link and transmitted. "This is R. Hunter, in the employ of the Governor Robot Oversight Committee. Respond, Mojave Center Governor component robot. We must discuss the danger to humans in the future." Then, as he waited for an answer, he explained to Jane what he was doing.

"Any answer?"

"Not yet," said Hunter. "Do you think he will answer?"

"Hard to say. From his point of view, you are introducing a rather vague First Law concern. It will be open to his interpretation."

"In what way?"

"If he feels that his own danger from us is more immediate than the theoretical danger he poses to humans in the future, then he may have the freedom of choice not to answer you."

"As a robot, I cannot give him a Second Law instruction," said Hunter. "But I suspect that he—I will call him MC 1—may have shut down his radio link to avoid receiving any transmission from me that might compel him to cooperate with us under the Laws of Robotics."

"I agree. As soon as he saw us, he must have known we were after him. Since the only radio transmission here would come from you or his own partner components, he won't need it for anything else."

"That does mean he will not try to coordinate with the others if they are here."

"True. In fact, he may very well have shut off his aural capability, at least within the sound range of human speech. That way no amount of shouting from us humans can force his obedience under the Second Law."

"Yes, I understand." Hunter listened again for some sound of MC 1 in the distance. Any number of large and small animals, presumably dinosaurs, were moving about in the forest within his hearing, but he heard no sounds that he could specifically identify as coming from MC 1.

"We could still try trapping him again," said Jane. "It simply requires staging a trap in his line of sight."

"The whole character of our search has to change," said Hunter. "We have no way of anticipating now where he will be at any given time. So even if we decide to use a trap to catch him, we have to find him first."

"Do you have a revised plan?"

"Maybe. Our new search has to be based on the fact that MC 1 is no longer miniaturized. My enhanced vision should be able to track him to some degree and my hearing may still reveal something, especially if I can detect a pattern to separate the sounds of his movements from those of dinosaurs." Hunter walked over to Chad.

The stegoceras was no longer struggling. It was now standing still, glaring suspiciously at all of them, effectively held in place by the two ropes around its neck. Chad was looking at it from several different angles.

"We no longer need it," said Hunter. "When you have finished gathering your data, we must free it unharmed."

"I'm finished," said Chad, nodding his agreement. "This is really exciting, Hunter. I have the first raw data ever gathered from a living dinosaur. In fact, I've taped him with the camera built into this belt computer."

Hunter moved to the nearest rope and untied it from the tree trunk. "Chad, what are the chances that we can actually rope and tame some dinosaurs to ride?"

"Ride?" Chad looked at him in surprise. "Uh—well, I'll have to think that over." He sat down on a large rock and consulted his belt computer again.

Hunter held the rope taut as he moved toward the stegoceras. When he reached it, the small dinosaur tried to butt him in the stomach. Hunter ignored the slight collision and released the other loop from its neck. Then he led the stegoceras away from the humans by the first rope.

"I will take him a short distance into the forest before I free him."

"I'll walk with you," said Jane.

As they picked their way through the forest, Hunter kept the stegoceras tightly leashed and away from Jane.

"I've been thinking," said Jane. "You should have a better chance of chasing down MC 1 on your own now."

"Maybe in the short term," said Hunter. "If I could catch him quickly."

"You know you can track him and keep up a pace of hiking and even running after him that we can't match. Since you're much bigger than the component robots, you can physically overpower him. You won't need us humans to give him Second Law instructions. Maybe we should just stay in camp, out of your way."

"That is one possibility I must consider," said Hunter, dragging the stubborn stegoceras after him on the rope. "However, the trail of MC 1 could lead me away from camp for a protracted period. I have to consider this environment largely unknown and potentially very harmful."

"In other words, you don't want to leave us alone." Jane ducked under a low-hanging tree branch.

"Not for very long. I cannot. If any of you humans remain in camp, the First Law will not allow me to leave you unsupervised for very long. That means I cannot go off on an open-ended chase. If I can arrange for you to come with me safely, then I can fulfill my First Law obligations to you while we are pursuing MC 1."

"I see. And if you and MC 1 start a footrace, the rest of us will need mounts to keep up with you."

"Yes." Hunter stopped. "I think I can let our friend go now. Please step behind me in case he is still angry."

"All right." Jane slipped behind Hunter, giving him some room to maneuver.

Hunter held the dinosaur's neck firmly in the crook of one arm while he took off the loop. Then he released the little stegoceras and stepped back warily. The dinosaur shook its domed head, glanced at him, and darted away through the thick underbrush. Still, Hunter listened to its footsteps until he was sure that the herbivore had truly lost interest in coming back to ram any of them.

"Gone?" Jane asked.

"Yes." Hunter turned to start back to camp. "He was too small for anyone to ride."

They walked back to camp in silence. By the time they arrived, Steve had erected a large, blue-domed tent. He had set up the portable kitchen and also arranged the sleeping bags inside the tent. Chad was leaning back against a tree, still working with his belt computer.

"I think our search for MC 1 may also involve a time limit of sorts," said Jane thoughtfully.

"A time limit? Of what sort?" Hunter had not been aware of any.

Chad looked up with interest. Steve also stopped working in order to listen.

"The miniaturization and subsequent reversal has almost certainly weakened MC 1's molecular structure, making him much more fragile than normal," said Jane.

"You think a fight with a dinosaur might destroy him?" Hunter asked.

"Possibly," said Jane. "But another problem is almost guaranteed."

"Another problem?"

"In this warm, humid climate, microscopic life must be very active," said Jane. "As long as MC 1 was microscopic himself, he was defending himself directly from other microbes—possibly even fighting with them under the Third Law. But now he's too big to do that."

"So the microbes are going to start interfering with his robotic body?" Hunter asked. "In a way that would not normally occur, without the effects of miniaturization and its subsequent termination?"

"Yes, little by little."

"I understand. If he falls down unseen here in this forest, he may be impossible to find. At the very best, it will take more sophisticated equipment than we have."

"I'm afraid so."

"Wait a minute," said Steve. "If the robot's dead, so to speak, then he won't be actively interfering with history. So we just have to catch the others, right?"

"No," said Hunter. "I cannot allow him just to remain here. According to chaos theory as applied to history, even his rusting, corroding remains could change some subtle part of human history in the far future."

"That seems hard to believe," said Steve.

Chad laughed. "You just don't understand the general principle of the theory."

"All right, then," said Steve. "Suppose you just tell me. How, here in the Late Cretaceous Period, can the body of one nonfunctioning robot possibly matter?"

"You ever hear of the term 'therapsids'?" Chad demanded with a smirk.

"No," Steve admitted.

"That word, my ignorant friend, refers to some mammal-like reptiles that lived long before even this period that we're in now. Generally, they were small, active, rather aggressive carnivores. All true mammals are descended from them—meaning that some of our very own human ancestors are alive right now, in one form or another. You follow me?"

"Yeah."

Chad grinned and gestured toward the surrounding forest. "All kinds of little critters are roaming around this forest. In fact, though it's unlikely—who knows?— one of the little local monsters might actually be our own *very* great grandma!" He laughed.

"So what does this have to do with a rusting robot?" Steve demanded.

"So dense." Chad rolled his eyes. "All right, look. That robot has compound substances in it that are modern industrial creations. They don't belong in this time. If some of our very distant human ancestors poison themselves trying to eat that stuff, they die early—and maybe they won't reproduce, or they may have chromosome damage that changes the traits of their offspring. Now do you see how human history could be changed by something like this?"

"Yeah, I guess, but it still sounds pretty farfetched," said Steve skeptically.

"Yes, statistically it is quite unlikely," said Hunter. "But not impossible. That is the problem that chaos theory presents me with under the First Law. The degree of probability that MC 1's permanent presence may harm all humans is still too great for me to accept."

Steve just shrugged.

"Chad," said Hunter. "What do you think about capturing some herbivorous dinosaurs we could ride?"

"Well, from what little information I have, I would say there's a reasonable chance."

"Can you recommend some likely species? Some that we can find in this forest?"

"Yes. That is, I can suggest some that appear to be a good size and shape to ride. But the fossil evidence can't possibly tell me something as subtle as how long a certain species might take for a rider to break."

"Understood," said Hunter. "We will be the first to give it a real try."

"What kind of dinosaurs have you picked?" Steve asked.

"What's your hurry?" Chad snickered.

Steve stiffened at his tone. "Nobody's going to break a new mount without equipment. If you want to ride a dinosaur, you—and all of us—will need some kind of stirrups and halter at the very least, preferably a bridle and a saddle if I can rig them up."

"An excellent point," said Hunter.

"So," said Steve, "I need to know the rough size and shape of the heads, necks, and torsos of the dinosaurs you expect us to ride. Then I can start checking our equipment for something we can use."

"All right," said Chad, now speaking in a normal tone of voice. "Here, take a look at this screen. Our first choice is going to be the struthiomimus.

It kind of resembles an ostrich."

Steve moved around and looked over his shoulder. "Two meters tall, three and a half meters long, head and neck like an ostrich. Got it."

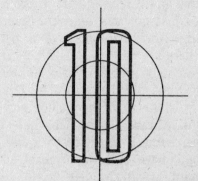

Steve eyed the sunlight that filtered brightly through a few gaps in the canopy of leaves overhead. The sun was low; only an hour or so of daylight was left. He made dinner with the supplies they had brought, using a small, portable electric stove.

The group sat in a circle outside the front of the tent, eating from biodegradable dishes and utensils. Steve, remembering his camping experience, had been thinking ahead. He was determined to show Chad that he knew what he was doing, at least within his own area of responsibility.

"This is going to take longer than you hoped, isn't it?" Steve asked Hunter, between mouthfuls.

"I believe so," said Hunter. "If the stegoceras had been under control when MC 1 appeared, I could have given chase at that time. Once he was out of my sight and hearing, though, the moment was past. From that point, a new plan was required."

"Hunter, we have water for only another twenty-four hours. Our food will last a couple of days if we ration it, but we can stretch it indefinitely if we do some hunting and gathering here in the forest."

"Why not just go back home for more supplies?" Chad asked. "Now that we have a better idea of conditions here."

"That presents a problem," said Hunter. "I have to conduct the time travel myself. The First Law stops me from leaving any of you alone for long and I would not dare leave any humans here without me. On the other hand, if we all go back and then return here, I would have to bring us back only seconds, or maybe minutes, after we left."

"Why?" Steve asked.

"Otherwise, the additional component robots might spring up from microscopic to normal size while we're gone and we would miss them, too."

"So what's the problem?" Chad shrugged. "You can arrange for us to come back here right after we left, can't you?"

"I do not dare cut it too close," said Hunter. "All kinds of theoretical paradoxes are possible in time travel. With a tight margin of error, it is possible that a mistake could bring us back a few seconds before we left, and we would meet ourselves. The potential harm is immense, and the First Law will not even let me consider that."

"Wait a minute," said Jane. "You still have to weigh the possible damage we will do to this time period if we start consuming resources."

"I have been making calculations about that," said Hunter. "No action is totally without risk, but I think that some careful hunting and gathering of food and water for a day or two will offer the least amount of risk."

Jane looked up from her dinner at him for a moment. "Are you sure that our eating some fish or reptiles won't set off a chain of events that totally changes our future? That is what the chaos theory is about, isn't it?"

"This is ridiculous," said Steve impatiently. "I can't believe that catching a couple of fish is going to end the world in our own time. This kind of talk drives me crazy." He got up and started gathering the empty dishes and cups.

Behind him, Hunter remained calm in the twilight.

"I have to take this possibility seriously," Hunter said. "However, I feel that consuming a small amount of food will do no more damage than staying here and stepping on the plants, climbing trees, or roping and riding dinosaurs. I do believe that we should catch fish, however, as opposed to dinosaurs or mammalian ancestors."

"What?" Steve turned around from the portable kitchen equipment. "You mean that eating a fish instead of a little dinosaur the same size might actually make a difference sixty million years from now?"

"The chance of making a significant change is less," Hunter said patiently.

Steve noticed that even Chad was listening attentively; apparently, this question wasn't as stupid as some of the others he had asked.

"Fish will continue to be a crucial part of the food chain," said Hunter. "And many species will continue to evolve. However, they will not play as crucial a role as dinosaurs and mammals will."

"Since the dinosaurs all die out later anyway," said Steve, "who cares if we eat a few now?"

"I cannot know particulars," said Hunter. "I am simply calculating the chances. An individual fish that you catch and eat is less likely to be important than an individual dinosaur or mammalian ancestor." He looked around at all of them. "If the most extreme form of chaos theory is true, then we have already made serious changes."

"Well." Jane smiled. "I wasn't crazy about eating a lot of giant lizard meat anyway."

Chad and Steve laughed.

"I will help Steve carry water from the stream," said Hunter. "We know the water has potentially dangerous microbes in it, so it will have to be boiled before you humans consume it in any form. Also, I will have to taste everything you eat from this environment first. Is that clearly understood and accepted?"

"Sure." Chad nodded.

"Wait a minute," said Steve. "I hate to be the only one asking all these questions, but you robots can survive all kinds of stuff that will kill humans. Just because some food doesn't make you malfunction won't mean it can't poison us."

"That's a reasonable question," said Jane.

"My taste sensors have the ability to study the chemical composition of substances," said Hunter. "I can judge whether comsuming something will kill a human, and the likelihood of its making one ill. Otherwise, the First Law would not allow me to let any of you eat an unknown food. Even certain kinds of fish can be poisonous. Naturally, even the food I judge to be edible will have to be fully cooked."

"I'm convinced." Steve grinned. "You won't catch me complaining about this."

"Chad," said Hunter. "How should we go about catching dinosaurs to ride?"

"Well, a snare is out," said Chad. "It might injure their legs and make them unfit for riding. I suppose we'll just have to lasso them somehow."

"We have rope for that," said Hunter. "What else?"

"We'll need a corral," said Steve. "To hold them, especially at first."

"A holding pen," said Hunter. "If I make one of wood, will it be strong enough?"

"I think it's worth trying," said Chad. "Our prospective mounts will certainly be strong enough to smash through wooden rails if they want."

"Then what good is a corral?" Hunter asked.

"Many animals won't try to break out unless they're really excited," said Steve. "Horses, for instance. They can often kick out of a wooden stall or corral if they want. But most of the time they don't bother."

"Exactly," said Chad. "I can't tell you what level of excitement dinosaurs would have to reach before they try it. I suppose each species of dinosaur might respond a little differently."

"Then I will try it," said Hunter. "This forest has plenty of fallen trees and standing dead ones. I can build a corral out of dead wood without killing any of the live trees."

"We can all help," said Steve.

"Not necessary." Hunter studied the forest immediately around them.

No one spoke. At first, Steve couldn't figure out why Hunter was looking around in the dark. Then he remembered that Hunter had infrared night vision and could see images in the dark because of the difference in the amount of heat radiated by various objects.

"The wood I need is close enough," Hunter concluded. "While you three are sleeping, I'll work on the corral. I will not need to rest. I have plenty of energy stored up. During the day tomorrow, my body's surface solar cells can replenish what I use tonight."

"I'm worried about the distance MC 1 can cover," said Jane. "Since we saw him, he's already had a number of hours to keep moving. Like you, he can move all night on stored energy and replenish it in the sunlight tomorrow."

"You mean he can stay on the run night and day?" Steve's eyes widened.

"That's right," said Jane. "He has an internal monitor like Hunter's, that tells him how much energy his body has in storage at any time. As long as he lets the sunlight restore as much or more than he uses, he can keep moving."

Hunter looked at Jane somberly. "I suggest we split up into teams tomorrow."

"Will the First Law allow that?" Jane asked.

"Only if everyone agrees to my conditions. Here is what I propose. During the night, I will build a small corral out of dead wood. If I am not finished by sunrise, Chad can help me finish it."

"What?" Steve looked at him in surprise. "Building the corral sounds more like my kind of work."

"Definitely," said Chad. "Why not have Steve do that with you?"

"Hear me out," Hunter said patiently. "After you and I have finished the corral, we will do some hunting. You will help me search for struthiomimuses, or other suitable dinosaurs, and we may fish in the stream as well."

"All right," said Chad. "You want me to help find certain dinosaurs; I understand. I still say Steve ought to work on the corral with you."

"I want Steve to help Jane track MC 1," said Hunter. "I have a small transmitter for one of you to carry. If you see any sign of trouble, you are to warn me instantly. If possible, you will hurry back to camp immediately. Otherwise, you take the safest course of action you can until I can reach you. Is this understood?"

"Of course," said Jane.

"Sounds good to me," said Steve. He grinned at Chad. They both knew that Hunter was sending Steve with Jane because he could handle the tracking and hiking better than Chad. Hunter was simply too tactful to say so.

"We'll have to look for signs of erratic behavior or physical change in MC 1," said Jane, "in addition to his choice of evasive pattern and his general direction. I doubt we can actually catch him without mounts, but I might find some behavior patterns that will help us anticipate his movements later."

"Excellent," said Hunter.

"Something you might think about," said Steve. "I can rig reins, bridles, and cinches out of rope. But if you can think of a way to make saddles, stirrups that will hold our weight if we stand, and bits that a dinosaur can't bite through, that will help."

"I will consider it," said Hunter. "May I ask if you are sleepy?"

All three of them laughed.

"Yeah, actually," said Steve. "I usually get up at dawn and go to bed shortly after dark. I'm ready for bed."

"Not quite yet for me," said Jane. "I'll just sit up and enjoy the evening."

"Me too," said Chad. "I'll look through my belt computer some more."

"Then I will start work on the corral," said Hunter, and he moved away into the darkness.

Steve brushed his teeth and washed up using a pan of water. Then he went into the tent and took off his boots. He slipped into one of the sleeping bags, where he relaxed for the first time since they had arrived in this time. While he certainly didn't like Chad much, he was enjoying the feeling of adventure. Tomorrow should be a real challenge.

When Steve woke up, Jane and Chad were still asleep in the tent. He quietly crawled outside into the cool, humid forest air. Shafts of bright light filtered through the trees overhead.

"Good morning, Steve," Hunter said quietly. He was about ten meters away from the tent.

Steve turned and stopped in surprise. Hunter was standing by a sturdy corral constructed of many different kinds of wood. It was unevenly shaped, the perimeter going around various trees and even enclosing a number of them.

"Do you think this will be adequate?" Hunter asked. "It is fifteen meters across at the narrowest and twenty at the widest. The gate is this bar in front." He patted the gate with one hand.

"It looks great," said Steve.

"I notched the logs to fit into each other," said Hunter. "But the rails are not really very sturdy. I do not have nails or the equipment to drill precise holes for dowels. I thought about lashing the junctures with vines, but that would mean killing living vines, which I consider unwise. Dead vines, of course, are too brittle."

"If a good-sized dinosaur really wanted to kick down the rails, nails and dowels wouldn't stop him," said Steve.

"Let me show you what else I made," said Hunter, moving to a pile of objects under a tree.

"I don't recognize this stuff," said Steve.

"Our storage cases had steel support bands," said Hunter. "I broke off some pieces. This one, for instance, I twisted into a short length to use as a bit. What do you think of it?"

"Oh! Of course." Steve took the piece of oddly-shaped metal. "It looks great for a horse. We'll have to find out if a dinosaur can bite through it or not. What's this other stuff?"

"Several more bits, of course." Hunter pointed to different items in the pile. "Those flat metal pieces should support your weight as stirrups."

"What about these big wooden things?"

"Those are rudimentary saddles," said Hunter. "I accessed data I had about old English riding saddles and modeled these on that design. They use less material than larger ones."

"Oh, yes. I recognize the shape now."

"I carved the top to fit human anatomy, of course. You will find metal bands in the bottom for connecting a girth and cinch. This design has no saddle horn."

"Very serviceable," said Steve. "I'll have to wait until we've caught a mount before I tie together a bridle or measure a girth. Otherwise, I can't estimate the sizes."

"Understood."

"How could you do all this work in one night?" Steve looked at Hunter in astonishment.

Hunter grinned. "It helps not to get tired. I do not need breaks and I did not slow down until the last hour before sunrise. At that point my stored energy was running low, but I am already replenishing it now that the sun has come up."

"We're practically in the shade here, Hunter."

"It is good enough."

"Even through your clothes?" Steve asked, grinning.

"My face and hands are exposed all the time." Hunter shrugged. "I will be fine soon. But you three will require breakfast. How much longer are Chad and Jane likely to sleep?"

Steve grinned. "I think they've had enough sleep. I'll start breakfast. Maybe they would enjoy being awakened by a loud shout from a robot."

"Really?" Hunter looked at the tent. "My experience with humans is still limited. I will try it."

Steve had breakfast ready by the time Jane and Chad were dressed and out of the tent. Soon enough, the team was ready to start the day. Steve wore a small day pack with food and water for them both. It was enough for them to stay out of camp until sundown.

"Here is the transmitter," Hunter said, handing Jane a tiny metal bead.

"It's turned on all the time?" Steve asked, studying the transmitter in Jane's fingers.

"Yes. It has no clip, so I suggest you button it securely in one of your pockets," said Hunter.

"All right." Jane did so.

"I will have my comlink fixed on your frequency," said Hunter. "It emits beeps at regular intervals, so I can track your position at all times. But I must trust you to call for help at the first sign of danger."

"We will," said Jane. "I'm ready."

"Have fun with the mighty forest hunter," Chad said snidely to Jane.

Ignoring Chad, Steve nodded to Hunter and led Jane to the spot where MC 1 had last been seen. He pointed to the faint footprints the robot had left. Jane nodded and followed him through the forest.

"Tracking is a lot easier out in the desert," said Steve, crouching low to study the ground again. "The soft sand retains clearer footprints."

"Will we be able to track him through the forest?" Jane asked. "Even after he quits running?"

"Yeah. It's just tougher." Steve fingered a broken twig. "An animal, say a dinosaur, could have done this. But it's a fairly fresh break, so it was probably made by MC 1." He reached up to a bigger branch and started to break it.

"Stop it! What are you doing?" She grabbed his wrist and pulled it away.

"I'm blazing a trail, so we can find our way back. We aren't going to find any road signs out here." He smiled and started to break the branch again.

"You can't!" She pulled his arm away. "Remember the historical theory Hunter talked about?"

"Aw, come on. You mean breaking a couple of branches is going to stunt human evolution forever?" He pointed in the direction MC 1 had taken. "What about him? He's snapping twigs every time he runs into a tree. And he's stomping on the grass—horrors! So are we!" He laughed, looking at the soft, cool turf under his feet.

"I know." Jane smiled patiently, but she kept her hold on his arm. "Yes, he's making small changes here. And we are, too. But it's important—very important, Steve—for us not to make any changes we can avoid."

"But breaking these twigs doesn't even kill the tree or the bush."

"I agree that it doesn't seem too serious," said Jane. "But the theory says that all changes keep expanding, like ripples in a pool of water. Maybe these twigs are going to drop specific seeds whose descendants will mutate in a certain way, or feed a certain animal. You see what I mean?"

"I guess."

"In fact, I'm afraid it's possible that the impact of our being here has already caused terrible harm to the time we come from."

Steve shook his head. "None of us should have come back here, including MC Governor."

"I don't blame you for not believing it," said Jane, releasing his arm. "These calculations are very complex and the theory requires a lot of abstraction. I'm sure you don't have much experience with this kind of thing."

"Thanks a lot." Steve pulled fully away from her. "You highly eduated geniuses can't even find your way around in nature after you leave an artificial environment. Come on, follow the desert rat."

He hurried away, looking up at the trees for unusual shapes and markings. As long as he was careful, he could keep track of their trail this way. Still, he wished they had landed in a desert, where his everyday habits from back home would have been more useful.

Hunter, continuously monitoring the beep from Jane's transmitter, generally trusted Steve's ability in the wild and knew he could track MC 1 better than the other two humans. Also, Hunter had teamed him with Jane in the belief that she was more compatible with him than Chad. Still, they might easily stumble across that velociraptor or another predator, and Hunter was worried that he was skirting the edge of the First Law by letting them go without him.

He kept all of these thoughts to himself, of course. His experience with humans was limited, but he had been programmed with certain basic data on human pyschology. He knew that they needed to have confidence in his leadership.

As Hunter reviewed these thoughts, he and Chad carried the water containers to the stream that Steve had found. They filled them and lugged the water back to the camp. Hunter bore most of the weight, but Chad insisted on doing his share.

Hunter had calculated before they had left that the three humans would require four and a half liters of water a day. As a humanoid robot, he needed a smaller amount, to replenish his simulated saliva and perspiration. Once the water had been stored in camp, he picked up some materials he could adapt for fishing. He and Chad returned to the stream, carrying their lassos.

The stream was only about a meter wide here, occasionally broadening into pools about twice that size. Hunter judged the average depth at one and a half meters; the water ran fast enough to be fairly clear. The heavy canopy of trees arched over it and the roots of thick trunks were exposed at intervals along the bank.

"My hearing is turned up," said Hunter. "It tells me that all kinds of animals are nearby in the forest. Have you seen any of them?"

"Only glimpses," said Chad. "I haven't had a good look at them. Can you tell from the sound if any of them are a good riding size?"

"Many of them are," said Hunter. "My concern under the First and Third Laws is that I cannot tell which ones are predators waiting for a kill and which ones are herbivores hiding from us in case we are the predators."

"In a sense we are," said Chad, grinning. "We're just not going to eat the ones we catch."

"True." Hunter nodded, not sure why Chad thought his comment was amusing. "I cannot see them well enough to pick out different species, either. As a paleontologist, what do you suggest as a course of action?"

Chad did not answer right away. He looked up and down the stream and around the forest. "You know, the animals here don't have the ingrained fear of humans that wild animals in our own time have. They're being cautious around us, but I think if we sit down quietly, maybe some of them will come into sight for a drink of water."

"Ah. A change in our approach sounds very good. Suppose we fish in the stream and see what happens around us."

"Fine."

"Here. This thread is quite strong. I pulled it out of the seam of one of the packs. That little buckle is also from the pack and will act as a sinker. You know how to use these?"

"Yes," said Chad. "I've read about fishing. What was this hook made from?"

"A latch on one of the storage cases. I twisted it into that shape."

"I see." Chad sat down on a rock near the edge of the water and carefully tied the gear together. "Say, what do I use for bait?"

"Oh, yes." Hunter looked around in the air for a moment. He spotted a couple of insects fluttering around a small bush. Slowly, he stepped toward them, raising his hand. Then, using his highly precise eye-hand coordination, he snatched one out of the air.

"Wow." Chad stared at him in shock.

"The local fish eat these all the time," said Hunter, as he tied the insect to the line just above the hook. "I judge that since we are taking the risk of fishing anyway, this is the best bait to use. If we use something we brought with us, and it affects the water or is taken by a fish that gets away, we do not know what consequence may result."

"I see," said Chad, gently lowering his line into the water with his hands.

"I will bring you a dead branch you can use for a pole," said Hunter.

"Thanks."

Hunter moved to a half-fallen dead tree. As he grasped a meter-long branch and gently ripped it from the trunk, he questioned his wisdom in bringing the human team with him. If he had come to this time period alone, he could simply be chasing down MC 1 this minute.

Of course, he reminded himself, if a direct physical pursuit had failed for some reason, he would still have wanted Jane's expert understanding of robotics and Chad's knowledge of dinosaurs. So that line of consideration merely took him in a circle. Returning the humans to their own time and coming back here alone would be no solution either.

Hunter returned to Chad, handing him the branch without a word. Chad tied the line to end of the branch carefully, then grinned up at Hunter. "Now I just wait. Did you bring fishing materials for yourself too?"

"No need, I believe," said Hunter. "I'll find out." He picked his way downstream several meters and then crouched on the bank. For a moment, he remained absolutely motionless except for his eyes as he watched dark shapes slipping lazily in the water below him.

Chad said nothing, watching him.

Once Hunter had studied the swimming motion and reflexes of the fish below him, he slowly moved his hand into the water and held it still. After a moment of warily darting away, the fish returned to their former movements. Then Hunter quickly reached down and grabbed one by the gills. In the same moment, he stood up, raising the wriggling fish out of the water and over the bank. It was big enough to eat.

"What do you think?"

"Wow," Chad said again.

For most of the day, Steve tracked MC 1 steadily through the forest. In some areas the tracks were very clear. Sometimes he had to stop and look closely. They ate lunch at midday and plodded on.

Late in the afternoon, Steve stopped and turned to Jane. "I don't know that we're accomplishing anything. Have you seen anything important?"

"We've been zigzagging and circling all day, haven't we?" Jane asked.

"Yeah, that's right."

"MC 1 isn't just running straight away, is he? For distance, I mean."

"Well—" Steve stopped, considering. "I guess he isn't. If we were chasing him with hounds, I'd say he was doubling back and crossing his own path to confuse the scent. But he must know that we didn't bring any hounds. So I'm not sure why he's doing this."

"I suppose he might access stored data about creating evasive patterns under certain conditions. The one truth about studying a robot's behavior is that it will be absolutely logical according to his own interpretation of his data and the Three Laws."

Steve nodded.

"Can you tell how old the track is?"

"No. If we were talking about a difference of a day or so, I might be able to. But we know he's been at normal size less than a day. I can't judge the age of these tracks in hours." He shrugged.

"I see."

"Well, he's still running." Steve pointed to the robot's footprints at their feet. "He's humaniform, so he runs with essentially the same motion as a human. See how the front of the footstep is deeper than the rest of it?"

"Yes. The heel mark hardly shows at all."

"His weight is all forward, meaning he's running, and the tracks we've seen show that he's been running

From the R. Hunter files

The now-famous prototype of the highly successful "Hunter" class robot first demonstrated his remarkable abilities in the Mojave Center Governor case. The following images are drawn from the Robot City archives of Derec Avery, the eminent historian on robotics.

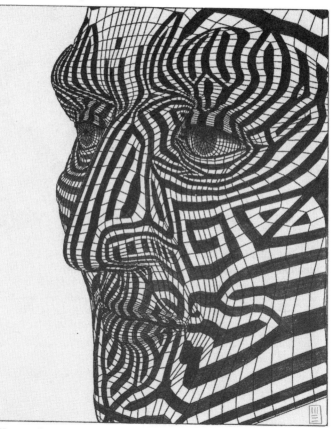

Hunter Sensenet Configured for Speech. Designed to hunt the missing Governor Robots, Hunter has a remarkable range of specialized abilities. He can alter his shape and size to adjust to different environments or cultures. Shown here is the sensory network underneath Hunter's skin when he is in speech-mode.

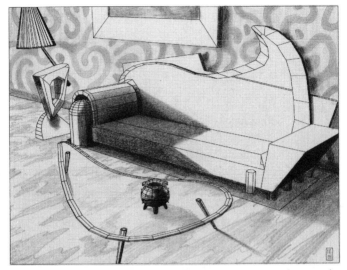

Mojave Center Governor's Waiting Room. Even in an underground city, robot labor allows for comfortable surroundings. This is the prototype city's Governor Robot waiting room, intended for humans who are waiting to see the Governor. Local humans and robots contact MC Governor directly or through his link to Mojave Center's main computer.

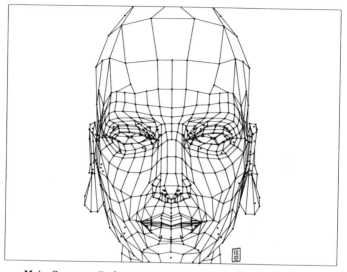

Main Sensenet Pathways in Governor Robot's Face. Designed to administer a major city and to cope effectively with any crises that city might encounter, Governor Robots contain multifunctional sensor arrays underneath their skin. These arrays tap the combined abilities of all six specialized positronic brains which combine to form a Governor Robot.

Mojave Center as Viewed from the Ridge near Steve's Home. Solar panels are the only surface sign of the prototype underground city. The ultramodern underground design relieves overcrowding while minimizing environmental impact.

Hunter Sensenet Configuration in Scan Mode. Underneath R. Hunter's skin is an advanced sensory network which augments his tracking and survival abilities. Hunter is capable of adjusting his sensitivity to outside conditions, increasing and decreasing sensory input in response to environmental conditions.

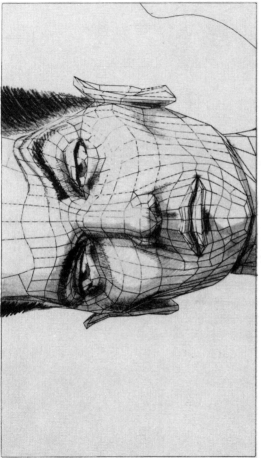

Mojave Center Governor. In its fully assembled state, the Governor Robot resembles an oversized humaniform robot. This simple exterior actually contains six separate robots, capable of combining their positronic brains to perform functions too complex for even the most sophisticated individual robots. Each of the six modules is also capable of functioning as a separate, highly-specialized robot.

Hunter on the Back of a Tyrannosaurus Rex. When the stampede backfires, Hunter desperately attempts to save his team from the most voracious of all dinosaurs.

Starting the Stampede. Steve, Jane and Hunter attempt to stampede a dinosaur herd to prevent MC1's escape.

Governor Robot Mitosis at Peak Polyfurcation. Governor Robo[
are capable of splitting into six separate, fully-functional robo[
each specializing in a particular area of local administration.

The Tower Containing Room F-12 at The Bohung Institute. The
Bohung Institute is the leading research facility in the underground city of Mojave Center. Room F-12 contains the miniaturization equipment which MC Governor uses to create a time-travel
mechanism.

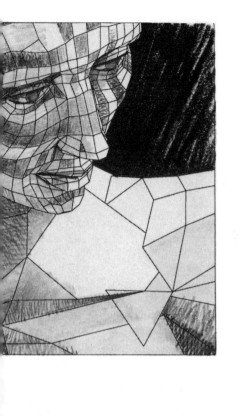

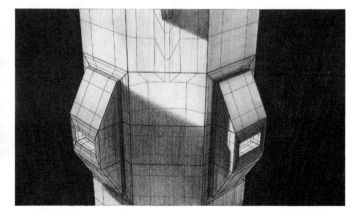

The Capture of the Struthiomimus. Hunter and his team must acquire fast mounts to capture the evasive MC1. Here, they lasso a small dinosaur.

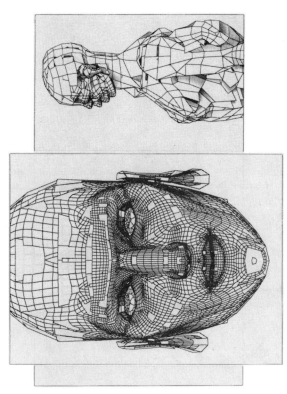

Governor Robot in the Early Stages of Neural Net Mitosis. The six separate positronic brains which give the Mojave Center Governor Robot its enormous administrative abilities are here seen in the process of separation into specialized modules/robots.

most of time. He seems to stop sometimes, maybe to get his bearings or to avoid a predatory dinosaur. Still, he's moving much faster than we are. We'll never catch him without those mounts."

"Well, didn't I say we shouldn't expect to? We came out here today to see what his habits are, that's all."

"Yeah, yeah, I remember," Steve said wearily. "But haven't you seen anything yet?"

"Well, I see that he's meandering all over the place. I just don't know what it means yet."

"Why not? You're the robotics expert, aren't you?" Steve grinned, wiping sweat from his forehead with the sleeve of his worksuit. "Isn't this why Hunter brought along a sheltered, pampered intellectual?"

Jane's face tightened. "It's a sure thing you can't figure out what he's doing."

"No one expects me to. In fact—" Steve stopped suddenly, looking at something ahead of them in the woods. He thought he saw two very human-looking eyes peering at him through the heavy foliage.

Jane looked too.

Suddenly MC 1 straightened up and slipped away through the underbrush.

"Stop!" Jane yelled. "I order you to stop! MC 1—Mojave Center component robot! You have to stop!"

"Come on!" Steve started after him, shoving through some branches.

"Stop!" Jane yelled again, hurrying after him.

Steve had to protect his eyes from the leaves and branches he plunged into, pushing them aside with both hands. In only a few steps, however, he realized that the robot was out of sight again. The footsteps were as clear as before, but MC 1 was running again. They couldn't possibly catch him.

Jane collided with Steve from behind.

"Take it easy," said Steve. "He's gone."

She nodded, panting. "He still must have his hearing turned off, as I said yesterday. The Second Law wouldn't have let him run away from me otherwise."

"He was watching us," said Steve. "He could be watching us right now."

"He can't hear us, though. He wouldn't dare risk it." Jane looked around, as if she could find him again. "I think that answers our question, though."

"Huh? Which one?"

"About his route. He isn't just trying to get away from us. I think his plan is to stay out of our control, but to keep an eye on us."

"You mean he's been watching us all day long?"

"I think so."

"Why didn't we see him before? Why now?"

"Chance, maybe," said Jane. "Or maybe he got a little careless after escaping our notice all day long."

"Yeah, maybe." Steve grinned. "If we hadn't followed him, he wouldn't have gone anywhere. We could have saved ourselves a day-long hike."

"Maybe so." She smiled.

He looked up at the sun through the trees. "Well, that discovery is worth something. But we're running out of daylight. Time to head back to camp while I can still remember the landmarks."

Hunter had caught and cleaned enough fish for the humans' next two meals during his first ten minutes of effort. Chad had taken his line out of the water, wryly observing that he was wasting his time. After that, the two of them had spent the afternoon sitting quietly, watching for dinosaurs.

When Hunter heard footsteps nearby, he quietly told Chad where to look. As they waited, they began to glimpse dinosaurs of all kinds up and down the stream, coming to the water to drink. The first one Hunter saw clearly was nearly five meters tall. It was a two-legged duck-billed creature, reaching up to munch on leaves as it worked its way toward the water.

Chad unclipped his belt computer, quickly punching in a description. "Small, bony crest on top of its head," he muttered. "Duckbill, small hump on its nose."

As Hunter watched, the dinosaur moved to the water and bent down low to drink. Its long tall flipped up slightly in the back to help it keep its balance. Another one, slightly shorter, appeared behind it.

"Brachylophosaurus," said Chad quietly. "Both of them. From the body type, I would say they aren't much good for riding. They run leaning forward, but stand up high when they reach for food. No matter how we arranged the saddles, we'd fall out when they shift up and down."

Hunter nodded. "Look downstream, on the opposite bank."

A low, four-legged dinosaur had just slipped from the underbrush to drink from the stream. Its pear-shaped head was fairly small, ending in a sharp beak. However, its body looked huge; most of it was still hidden by the forest cover. What Hunter could see was covered with rows of thick, bony plates. Long spikes protected its sides and shoulders.

"Panoplosaurus," Chad whispered, consulting his belt computer again. "Up to five and a half meters long, between two and three tons in weight."

"From the length of its legs, I would say it couldn't move fast enough to catch MC 1," Hunter observed.

"I wouldn't want to sit on one, anyway," said Chad, with a grin.

As the day wore on, the majority of dinosaurs that came to the water were varieties of hadrosaurs, such as the brachylophosaurus, according to Chad. He eagerly identified all the different species, which varied in size and color. They had duckbills and crests of different shapes on top of their heads. The legs of the hadrosaurs were strong and heavy, ending in three-toed, hooved feet. Their forelimbs were medium-sized, with webbed, four-fingered hands. Chad quickly entered all the new details that he could see.

"They are remarkably unconcerned with our presence," said Hunter. "My information on wild animals tells me that they are usually afraid of humans."

"The remaining wild animals in our own time are descended from very wary, suspicious ancestors who managed to avoid being hunted and fished by humans for many generations," said Chad, looking around for more dinosaurs.

"You think their behavior has changed through a form of selection, then."

"Well, these dinosaurs don't have any particular fear of us because humans have never existed around them before. They don't even know what to think of us. I guess as long as we sit quietly, the herbivores will just keep their distance and get their drink of water."

"Perhaps so."

"None of the hadrosaurs are good for riding," Chad said. "We need another type."

"I think I hear a new pattern of footsteps," said Hunter, suddenly lowering his voice. "Closer to that of the stegoceras, but of a larger beast. Look upstream, on this side."

They remained silent for a moment. A dinosaur's dark green head appeared through the leaves. It moved slowly, looking around. Then it leaned down to drink from the stream.

"Another velociraptor?" Hunter whispered.

Chad shook his head. "No, it's just very similar in appearance. That's the struthiomimus we've been looking for."

"Wait here." Hunter took his lasso from his shoulder. "I can move more quietly, I think. I will circle behind him and lasso him. Be ready to jump up and run to me. We will need both loops on him."

Chad nodded.

Hunter shifted into a very detailed sensory mode, in which he used his eyesight to analyze the plants and soil on the ground and the branches in front of him. With his instant reflexes, he judged exactly where to place his feet and how to move through the branches and leaves with maximum stealth. He only had to walk slightly more slowly than usual to do this. A human would have had to slow down considerably.

The struthiomimus drank from the water, then lifted its head on its very long neck to listen. Hunter stopped. When it lowered its head to drink again, he moved forward.

Hunter came up behind it. The struthiomimus was a two-legged dinosaur about two meters tall. Its neck represented almost half its total height. Hunter adjusted the loop on his lasso and waited.

The biggest problem in throwing the lasso was not just missing the dinosaur, but having tree branches get in the way. Hunter carefully studied the small clear area through which he could make his toss. He was ready by the time the struthiomimus finally turned away from the stream, back toward him.

Hunter judged the precise moment to throw his loop and tossed it with his finest control. As the struthiomimus turned to look at the movement of the rope, the loop fell over its head and all the way down its neck. The dinosaur pulled back, turning to run.

"Now!" Hunter shouted, flinging the free end of his rope around a tree. He wound it around the big tree trunk once, just before the fleeing dinosaur pulled the rope taut. Then Hunter hung on to the rope, using the tree trunk as a brace.

"I'm coming!" Chad ran crashing through the underbrush, swinging his lasso.

"This way," Hunter called. "Hold this rope and give me your lasso."

"I'll do it!" Chad dodged around a couple of trees and moved toward the struthiomimus, which was trampling the bushes and crashing against the trees in an effort to pull away.

"Stop!" Hunter screamed frantically. "It's too dangerous!"

"It's okay! He's already roped." Chad slowed down, approaching the raging dinosaur.

Hunter couldn't allow Chad to go any closer. Impelled by the First Law, Hunter quickly tied his rope into a knot and ran after Chad. "Chad, you must stop!"

The struthiomimus was straining its narrow neck against the rope, too panicked to pay any attention to Chad. Its heavy body was snapping young trees in half and its feet were flattening the underbrush. Chad, showing more courage than common sense, stood his ground and reared back to throw his lasso.

Hunter saw that Chad was close enough to be trampled if the terrified dinosaur suddenly shifted in his direction. To move him as fast as possible, Hunter flung himself forward in a flying tackle carefully gauged to bring Chad down without hurting him by the impact. He grabbed Chad around the waist, then turned so that as they hit the ground, Hunter's body cushioned Chad's.

"Stay there," Hunter ordered, leaping up and snatching away the rope. "If you do not keep yourself safe, I will have to cut it free so it cannot hurt you."

Chad just nodded.

Hunter moved up on the dinosaur quickly. This time, with its movements confined, lassoing it was even easier. Hunter tied the second rope securely to another tree and returned to the first rope to tie it more securely. The struthiomimus pulled against the ropes, but Hunter could see that they would hold.

"Now what do we do?" Chad had stood up now, but dutifully remained where Hunter had told him to stay.

"When he calms down, we have to move him to the corral," said Hunter. "How long do you think that will take?"

"What do I think?" Chad shook his head. "Nothing in the fossil record can predict his emotional state. All we can do is wait and see what he does."

"All right." Hunter looked through the trees in the direction of the camp. "We are not strong enough to pull him by hand in any direction he does not want to go."

"Then how do we make him come with us?"

"When he is calm, I will untie one rope at a time. While he is braced by the other rope, we will pull him or coax him with food to follow us. Then we will retie the lead rope to a tree trunk and do the same with the other one. The tree trunks are close enough for us to move him that way."

"That could take a long time."

Hunter looked up at the sun. "We have several hours of daylight."

Steve and Jane returned to camp first. When the setting sun turned red, Steve began preparing dinner. Even when it was ready, Hunter and Chad still had not returned.

"Maybe Hunter should have given us a receiver," said Jane. "So we could keep tabs on him, too."

Steve glanced over at her. She smiled impishly. He wasn't sure if she was serious or not. Ever since they had bickered a little out on the trail, he had been uncomfortable with her, but she seemed to have forgotten about it.

"Steve! Jane!" Hunter's voice came out of the darkening forest, not far away.

"Yeah!" Steve shouted back.

"Open the corral!"

Steve and Jane glanced at each other, then hurried toward the gate. They opened it. Then, out of the shadows, Hunter came into sight, pulling a taut rope.

"Ready, Chad?" Hunter called. "Untie your rope and hold it this time. We have to bring him into the corral." He turned to Steve. "Help Chad on his rope."

Steve and Jane jogged forward. They could hear something large breaking branches as it struggled. It was still invisible in the darkness.

"Steve? Over here," said Chad.

Steve looked around and saw him only a few steps away. As Chad loosened his rope from a tree, Steve grabbed it. So did Jane. Then, for the first time, Steve saw the long neck and narrow head of the dinosaur, rising up high overhead.

"Just pull him," said Chad. "He's more docile now. He fought hard at first, but he's getting tired, I think."

"Okay."

Hunter pulled the hardest. Little by little, the dinosaur stepped forward, forced to move by the tautness of the two ropes around its neck. In a few moments Hunter and the three humans had all backed into the corral. The dinosaur, looking around in jerky, sudden movements, at last stepped inside the corral gate.

Hunter quickly lashed his rope to one of the trees inside the corral. Then, circling safely around the dinosaur, he took the rope from Chad. "Climb over the rails," he said. "Stay away from the struthiomimus."

Steve dropped the rope and moved toward the fence. He clambered over the rails first and turned. Jane leaned down to brace herself on the arm he offered. Chad climbed over slowly at another part of the fence.

In the corral Hunter held the rope firmly as he backed to the fence. Then he let go of it and carefully watched the dinosaur. The struthiomimus, feeling the release of tension, suddenly pranced sideways. At the same time, Hunter dodged behind it and moved to the other rope. He untied it and then ran to the nearest part of the fence, where he jumped over.

The dinosaur began to run around the corral, among the trees.

"Get away!" Hunter yelled at the humans, seeing where they were. "Away from the fence. He might break out."

Steve backed off, but Hunter was frantically running toward them.

"Now! Move!" Hunter spread his arms wide, slowing down abruptly. He herded the three humans away from the fence, back toward the camp. "Stay behind me."

As they watched, the struthiomimus ran among the trees, shaking its head. For a moment it slipped out of sight in the dark, but reappeared, walking more slowly. So far it was still in the corral.

"It's really pretty calm for a wild animal in captivity," said Steve.

"It fought hard at first," said Hunter. "It quickly tired itself out pulling against the trees we used as braces. It may still break out sometime tonight."

"What do we do now?" Jane asked.

"Dinner's ready," said Steve. "Let's give our captive time to adjust."

"Yes," said Hunter. "I will listen carefully to the dinosaur's footsteps. If it becomes agitated, I will have to tend to it."

"I'm hungry enough," said Chad.

They sat down to eat facing the corral. By that time the forest was almost completely dark, but Steve moved one of the portable lights to the edge of the fence and angled it inside. They could see the dinosaur pacing anxiously among the trees, in and out of the light.

"Looks good so far," said Steve, as he collected the empty dishes. He began cleaning the fish that Hunter had brought back, intending to use them in a future meal.

"He's eating leaves," said Jane. "Look."

"That's a good sign," said Chad. "He's not as upset as he was. Maybe he won't break out."

"You three go to bed," said Hunter. "I will have to watch him all night. I cannot take the risk that he might break out and trample the tent."

"What if he does escape?" Steve asked. "What can you actually do about it?"

"I will retrieve the ropes now. If I anticipate that he will break out, I can tie him to a tree again."

"That's good enough for me," said Jane.

In the early light, Steve again woke up first. He hurried out right away to take a look at the dinosaur. "Hey, Hunter! Is it still here?"

"Good morning, Steve," Hunter called from the corral. "Over this way."

Steve ran to the gate, then stopped in surprise. Hunter, riding on the back of the struthiomimus with a saddle and bridle, guided his mount from the trees into full view. He rode up to the gate as Steve stared.

"You can ride it already?" Steve gazed at the calm struthiomimus. "It really looks like an ostrich, doesn't it?"

"Yes, it does," said Chad, coming up behind Steve. "It's no accident, either. Walking birds in our own time, such as ostriches and emus, are among the closest living relatives of dinosaurs."

"Really? Are they descendants of dinosaurs like this one?" Steve asked.

"The answer to that is still being debated," said Chad. "Some experts say they are. Others feel that birds are descended from an ancestor common to the dinosaurs. That would make them descendants of, you might say, dinosaurs' cousins."

Steve nodded, impressed with Chad's knowledge. That was the most civil conversation he and Chad had yet exchanged. He didn't want to ruin it, so he said nothing else.

Hunter had used a small bit to go into the mouth of his mount and had tied a small bridle together out of rope. The struthiomimus's head was higher than Hunter's, and Hunter had to guide him with long reins. He sat on the small makeshift saddle, which was tightly cinched around the creature's body.

"How did you tame him so soon?" Chad asked.

"After he calmed down, he became very responsive to me," said Hunter. "I fed him with certain leaves and he let me get close. Since Steve needed his sleep, I spent a couple of hours making the saddle and bridle."

"Wait a minute. You mean he just let you ride him?" Steve asked doubtfully.

"No, not exactly. He did not like the saddle or bridle much at all. I had to tie him up again to put them on and he fought them for another couple of hours after I untied him."

"He got used to them pretty fast," said Chad. "Maybe he's smarter than the experts thought."

"I judge him to be somewhat less intelligent than a horse," said Hunter.

"How long have you been riding him?" Steve asked.

"About three hours," said Hunter. "The first time, I had to sneak up on him and jump on. The Third Law allowed this, because falling from this height is not too serious. I can control my falls."

"And now he's trained enough to ride," said Chad. "That's pretty good work."

"At least for the moment," said Hunter. "He may resist again if I get off."

"He's day-broke," said Steve.

"What?" Hunter asked.

"A horse that has to be broken to ride every day is called 'day-broke.'"

"I see. Yes, I think that is what he is," said Hunter. "However, to keep him under control, I should stay mounted on him through the day unless a more pressing concern develops."

"Okay," said Steve. "I'll get breakfast going right away. But then what do we do?"

"I want you to make another saddle for Chad," said Hunter. "One we can strap on behind mine up here. He will ride double with me. Also another bridle that he will use tomorrow if all goes well. Now that we have one mount to ride, we should be able to run down another struthiomimus fairly easily."

"Hey, that's right," said Chad. "No more sitting around waiting. And we won't have to drag it on foot with ropes either."

"What about Steve and me?" Jane asked, joining them at the corral.

"In the excitement last night, I never asked you for a debriefing," said Hunter. "What did you find?"

"MC 1's trail is all over the place," said Jane. "He's roaming, not just running. Steve did a great job of tracking him."

"Can you infer his motives?"

"Well, maybe. I've been thinking about it. Since he's not trying to put simple distance between himself and us, two general possibilities present themselves. One is that he has malfunctioned in some way. A physical malfunction may have impaired his ability to judge what he is doing and where he is going."

"He has no trouble running," said Steve. "He can move fast. We even glimpsed him once, watching us."

"That brings me to the second possibility," said Jane. "He may have some reason for staying close and watching us, even though that means greater risk for him."

"I would like you to continue tracking him today," said Hunter. "I hope that tomorrow we will have two mounts on which to follow him, so tomorrow morning we will want to pick up his trail in the most recent spot you can give us."

When breakfast was finished, Steve provisioned a day pack for Chad, cooking some of the fish and making sandwiches. Then he prepared the new saddle and bridle. Soon everyone was ready.

Steve handed Chad his pack and carried the saddle inside the corral. While Hunter held his mount steady, Steve, tingling with excitement, swung the new saddle up onto the back of the struthiomimus. He was ready to jump aside and run for the corral fence at the first sudden movement.

Hunter held the dinosaur firmly in place. Without incident, Steve cinched the saddle tight and waved to Chad, who was waiting at the gate. Then Chad, carrying the bridle, reluctantly came forward. Steve gave him a leg up into the saddle.

"Wow," Chad said quietly, settling into the saddle. "I'm actually riding a dinosaur."

"Put your arms around me and hang on," said Hunter. "Its gait is reliable, since it walks on only two legs. But it moves its head up and down on that long neck to eat and to look around. The body angle shifts a little at the same time."

"Right," said Chad, looking up at the struthiomimus's head with a new interest.

Steve ran to open the gate. Steve and Jane watched as the others rode out of the corral. Then, with a hesitant but controlled walk, Hunter and Chad's mount carried them into the forest.

"So far, so good," said Steve.

"They'll be fine," said Jane. "You know Hunter can't let either one of them get hurt if he can help it."

"Yeah, I know," said Steve. "I just hope he knows what he's doing."

Steve prepared their day pack and they started out again on foot. He followed his landmarks back to their terminal point of the day before. They picked up the trail again, still wandering through the dense forest on a curving, crisscrossing route.

After only an hour or so, Steve stopped for a moment. "This is silly. He's not going anywhere. Neither are we. We were in this spot twice yesterday and now today."

Jane looked down at the tracks, which were thick here. "Is he slowing down? Are those walking tracks instead of running tracks?"

"Yeah." Steve grinned at her. "You're learning."

"What I said yesterday goes double today. He really isn't trying to escape at all."

"No, I'd have to agree with you." Steve studied the footprints around them. "If he wanted to lose us, he could be wading up or down that stream. Then he wouldn't leave any trail at all. Or he might find some rocky ground somewhere."

"Yesterday, I thought he was just circling back to watch us. But he's not just doing that, either, or he would leave even less of a trail, don't you think?"

"That would make sense," said Steve. "But I'm just here to track our quarry through the forest. You're the expert on how robots think."

"I guess we'll just have to keep following him," said Jane. "But I wish I knew why he was hanging around like this."

"This way," said Steve.

Hunter rode for the first hour or so, giving most of his attention to his mount. The First Law had him deeply concerned about letting Chad ride with him. Finally, however, Hunter concluded that the dinosaur was truly under enough control for them to ride safely.

"I'd like to name it 'Strut,' " said Chad happily, over his shoulder. "A mount should have a name. Besides, 'struthiomimus' is just too long a word to say all the time."

"Strut," said Hunter. "Very well."

"I thought that was kind of funny. Don't you think that's a good name?"

"Short, distinctive, and a mnemonic for the species," said Hunter. "Yes, it is an appropriate name."

"And it walks upright."

"Yes?"

"You don't have much sense of humor, do you?"

Hunter quickly searched his data on the subject. He recalled that humor was important to humans. However, with the urgency of finding MC Governor or his components, Hunter had never taken the time to consider the subject.

"I apologize," said Hunter.

"No need." Chad laughed. "Never mind."

Puzzled, Hunter simply nodded.

Throughout midday, Hunter guided their mount quietly through the forest, looking for another struthiomimus. They could not find one. Hunter stopped at several places along the stream, where they waited again for dinosaurs to come to drink. Whenever a new species appeared, Chad quickly looked up its name and traits, but they did not see a specimen they could ride. So Hunter moved on.

Behind him, Chad ate his lunch as they rode. When he had finished, Hunter passed him the reins so that he could learn to ride Strut on his own. Hunter remained in the forward saddle, but that seemed to make no difference. Chad guided their mount without a problem.

"I've been looking in my belt computer for more species that might be good prospects," said Chad. "Maybe the struthiomimus just isn't common in this neighborhood right now."

"What data were you checking?"

"Only a few traits." Chad relaxed the reins so that their mount could crane its long neck forward to browse on some leaves. "Cranial capacity, for learning ability. Size and strength of leg bones, to make sure they can carry us. The structure of the pelvis and spine of bipedal dinosaurs, to judge whether or not they are likely to bend far forward and then straighten up suddenly again, throwing us."

"What have you found?"

"Well, so far, not much—"

Hunter held up his hand for silence. His hearing had just detected movement ahead. The four footsteps he heard sounded like those of something very heavy. At the same time, he heard the faint swishing and snapping of twigs—many of them at once, suggesting massive size to match the great weight of the creature.

Hunter waved his hand forward.

Chad urged the struthiomimus to walk. At first it moved casually enough, but then it suddenly stopped and turned its head in the direction of the animal Hunter had heard. Chad had to kick its body to urge it forward again.

Then Hunter got his first glimpses of the big dinosaur's body, though its head was still out of sight. It was roughly seven meters long and the curve of its back was nearly three meters from the ground. From the sound of its patient footsteps, he judged its weight at over four tons.

Behind Hunter, Chad drew in his breath sharply. Hunter felt a tap on his left shoulder. He looked and saw the creature raise its head.

The dinosaur had a short, thick nose horn and two long brow horns about a hundred centimeters long, curving forward. Its beak was turtlelike in shape. A smooth, solid frill covered the back and sides of its neck.

"A triceratops," Chad whispered.

"Is it ridable?" Hunter asked softly.

"I'm not sure. It's an herbivore and it's four-legged—and much too heavy to rear up."

"Obviously strong enough," said Hunter. "It does not look as though it can run fast."

"Not for very long, probably," said Chad. "But if you can ride it, you can probably chase MC 1. The real problem is that they were—are, that is—aggressive."

"How aggressive?"

"No one really knows. It might be like trying to tame and ride a rhinoceros."

Hunter reviewed his data. "I do not know much about those, either. Is that difficult?"

"Uh—the Third Law probably wouldn't allow it."

"I see." Hunter adjusted the coil of rope on his shoulder as he watched the triceratops calmly eating the leaves from a large, full bush. "Chad, can you ride Strut alone now?"

"Alone? I suppose so."

"I think you will be safe enough. Also, I believe we have left MC 1 alone too long. We must get on with our pursuit under the general First Law imperative. That requires that I take a chance under the Third Law." Hunter suddenly reached up to a strong overhead branch and swung out of the saddle.

Chad gasped in surprise, but kept Strut reined.

Hunter pulled himself up into the tree. "Be careful," he whispered. "Stay close if you can, but ride back to camp if you have to. You know the way?"

"Yeah. The stream is directly behind us and I can find the camp from there."

Hunter nodded. Then, taking great care to move quietly and safely, he climbed higher into the tree. When he could, he moved to a branch on a nearby tree, closer to the triceratops. He was going to climb right above it, where a certain branch angled over its frill.

Hunter reached that branch and swung out below it over the big dinosaur, moving forward hand over hand. With each arm movement, his weight shook the branch, rattling the leaves. The triceratops twitched its ears curiously but otherwise did not move from the bush it was eating. Assessing its massive build and heavily armed head and neck, Hunter judged that it was simply not concerned with anything small enough to climb trees.

When Hunter was hanging directly over the back of the dinosaur's frill, he let go with his right hand and slipped the coil of rope down his arm. Still hanging by his left hand, he shook the loop loose and tossed it downward, toward the right brow horn of the triceratops. A second later, he dropped onto the creature's back.

The shock of Hunter's weight landing on the triceratops made it jerk in surprise. Then it lumbered forward, crashing through bushes and flattening some of the smaller trees. Hunter leaned forward and grabbed the left brow horn in his free hand, bracing his right hand with the taut rope. He gripped the dinosaur's broad body with his legs as hard as he could and kept his head low as he rode the triceratops through the forest.

Steve and Jane returned to the camp first. As they walked out of the forest into the clearing, however, Steve stopped in alarm. The tent had collapsed. The sleeping bags were lying askew out on the ground and containers of food and equipment were spread around, some of their contents spilled out.

"What happened?" Jane asked, startled.

"Careful," said Steve quietly. "Maybe the scent of the food attracted some dinosaurs."

"I don't see any. They must have gone."

"Not all dinosaurs are real big. Some smaller ones might still be roaming around. Let's go slowly."

"All right."

Steve moved up first, warily circling the tent and scattered belongings. Jane followed him. Finally, satisfied that the intruder or intruders had gone, he relaxed.

"Tell me," said Steve, plodding wearily back to the tent and slipping the day pack to the ground. "Did we do anything today that was different from yesterday?"

He started gathering up containers and checking the contents.

"Not much, I admit," said Jane. "We were able to mark the latest tracks of MC 1, though."

"What for? So we can do the same thing tomorrow? This is pointless."

Jane sighed, nodding agreement. She picked up some of the equipment too. "It only means something if we start chasing him for real."

They both turned as Chad rode into view. The front saddle was empty. He glanced around the camp.

"What a mess. Is Hunter back?"

"No," said Jane. "What happened to him?"

"He jumped on a triceratops," said Chad. "I was so suprised, I never had a chance to try to talk him out of it."

"Really?" Steve grinned, amazed. "Even *I* know what that is. Wow."

"The next thing I knew, it ran off with him. That was hours ago. I followed him for a while; that triceratops left a trail smashing through the forest that nobody could miss. But then I thought maybe Hunter had gotten off at some point and would just walk back to camp."

"He hasn't been here," said Steve. "Unless you think the triceratops trampled everything here."

Chad rode closer. "What kind of tracks have you found?"

"I haven't looked yet." Steve looked down at the ground. In most places, footsteps had left only dull impressions in the heavy sod, revealing very little. In a muddy spot, however, he saw a heel print.

"That's no dinosaur," said Jane, joining him. "And it's too small to be Hunter's."

"It must be MC 1," said Steve. He walked quickly back to the tent and the spilled containers. "Definitely. Some of these lines were actually untied, not just broken or pulled down. And no dinosaur could have unlatched these containers. Our salt and flour were opened and poured onto the ground, but nothing is actually broken."

"I'm going to dismount in the corral," said Chad. "Be right back." He turned and rode away quickly.

"Now I have the answer to the question that was bothering me," said Jane.

"Which one?"

"Why MC 1 was hanging around, evading us but never really running away."

"What? You think he just wanted to trash our camp?" Steve bent down to pick up a few more items and set them upright. "He could have done it yesterday, but he didn't."

"It's more than that, Steve. He wants to disrupt our search. Yesterday he probably studied our habits to figure out how he would do it."

"So he's trying to chase us away?"

"To discourage us, at least. He has an insurmountable problem, however. The First Law won't let him do anything even potentially harmful to us humans, such as poisoning our food and water, or sabotaging our equipment."

"Say, that's right. But he dumped some food out onto the ground."

"He knows we won't eat it if we can see it's not safe anymore. And I bet he left us enough so that we won't starve. He can't take that chance, either."

Steve glanced into a few more containers. "Yeah, he did. We're still okay."

"He can't even set traps for us or take our supplies away. He has to leave us everything we need to remain safe." Jane smiled wryly. "In a way, I feel sorry for him. He's trying to do the impossible."

"Yeah, I see." Steve squinted toward the reddening sunlight filtering through the trees. "It's too late in the day to track him now. At least tomorrow we can start following him from right here."

"What a mess," said Chad, joining them from the corral. He winced as he walked. "Riding that struthiomimus is fun, but I'm saddle sore."

Jane laughed. "But you're the first human ever to ride a living dinosaur. For a paleontologist, that's quite a distinction, isn't it?"

"Yeah! I love that part." He grinned, then looked past her toward the trees. "Hey, there's Hunter now."

"Hunter!" Jane called.

"You okay?" Steve asked.

"Yes, yes." He hiked briskly toward them. "I am fine; no damage."

"What happened, Hunter?" Chad asked. "I followed you for most of the day, or at least I followed the triceratops. Then at sundown I figured I'd better get back to camp."

"I am glad you did," said Hunter. "It means I can trust you to take care of yourself under my First Law responsibilities. As for myself, I rode the triceratops for quite a long time. It does not buck or roll over on its back, so I just hung on."

"Then what happened?" Steve asked.

"It was a stalemate." Hunter shrugged. "I was not

strong enough to steer it by pulling on the brow horns and it could not get me off by charging around through the trees, as long as I stayed low. Finally I decided that I just was not accomplishing anything and jumped off." He studied the camp behind them. "Did this happen while everyone was gone?"

"Yes, we had a visitor," said Jane.

"So I see," said Hunter. "What happened?"

"MC 1," said Steve. "He left his tracks."

Hunter studied the damage. "Not too serious, I see. But I think the delay in our direct pursuit of him has lasted long enough. I will have to alter my priorities after all. Tomorrow morning I will chase him on foot alone."

"You and I can ride after him," said Chad. "If you're willing to leave all three of us on our own, then you can leave them and take me again."

"I will be more efficient alone," said Hunter. "And I will feel less pressure under the First Law if you three humans are together."

"Wait a minute," said Chad. "Why?"

"Then only one danger, if any, is likely to approach you. When you divide up, the chance of your encountering harm increases. Since I have only the one transmitter to warn me of danger to you, I must ask all three of you to wait here in camp for me tomorrow. Be ready to call me through the transmitter at the slightest hint of possible harm."

"All right," said Jane. "If this arrangement will help you track down MC 1 and grab him, then we can all go home sooner this way."

"I could use a break from all this hiking around for no particular reason," said Steve. "But right now I want to get dinner going."

"The rest of us will help put the camp back into shape," said Hunter.

"Good idea," said Jane.

Chad hesitated, but when Hunter and Jane began raising the tent, he joined the manual labor. Steve grinned to himself, but said nothing. He made dinner with more of the fish that Hunter had caught.

As the humans ate and relaxed afterward, Hunter finished putting the camp back into shape. He was now eager to get on the trail of MC 1 himself, feeling that delaying to capture mounts might have been a mistake. However, he knew he could not set out tonight.

The day's effort to ride the triceratops had used up too much of his energy. He did not have enough stored up to remain fully active until sunrise, when the light could replenish it. If he chased MC 1 during the night until his energy ran out, then stopped to wait for dawn, he would have none to use in the event of a First Law emergency at the camp. Besides, while the humans slept, they could be surprised by some problem that would prevent them from calling him on the transmitter.

Hunter sat down outside the tent. He stayed motionless in order to store his remaining energy, but kept his mind alert and all his sensors active to detect the sounds, sights, smells, and vibrations that would mean another visitor. If either MC 1 or any animal approached, he would still have enough energy to protect the humans.

In the morning, as soon as Hunter heard Steve stir in the tent, he returned to full activity. The dawn light was speckling the camp through the trees overhead. Hunter inspected the line of tracks that led away from camp.

"Hi, Hunter," said Steve, as he came out of the tent. "You about ready to go?"

"Yes. Before I left, I wanted to make sure that at least one of you was awake to call me on the transmitter in the event of trouble."

"Well, here I am."

"Yes. There you are." Hunter hesitated, not sure if this was a form of farewell or not. When Steve began inspecting the breakfast materials, Hunter decided that it was. He turned to the tracks and stored a careful visual memory of them. Then he set off at a jog.

As he made breakfast, Steve watched the struthiomimus with curiosity. It was wandering around the corral in apparent contentment, eating leaves from the trees. After breakfast Chad and Jane joined him in a walk to the corral, where they watched Strut in his temporary home.

"Quite a creature," said Jane. "The resemblance to an ostrich really is very strong."

"Yes," said Chad. "It was odd riding it, but I got used to it fast enough."

"So what do you think about all these dinosaurs now?" Steve asked.

"What do you mean?"

"Well, before we got here, everything you knew about dinosaurs came from fossils and guesswork. Now you've seen them for real. What do you think?"

"I wouldn't say it was guesswork," Chad said huffily. "Paleontologists have been studying fossil remains and living entities for years with great care. We've figured out all kinds of things through more than guesswork."

"All right, all right. But have you learned anything new since we've been here?" Steve demanded impatiently.

"Well, of course I have! We can surmise the color of some dinosaurs from their environment, and the kind of camouflage they must have needed—but now I know for sure what color some of them were."

Steve was getting angrier by the moment. "Yeah? And how did you know what kind of environment they lived in from only a bunch of fossils?"

"From where they're found," Chad snapped. "We can tell from the kind of rock they're in. To me, a fossil in sandstone means that the specimen died in water. The overall shape and other nearby fossils will tell me if it was a streambed or an ocean. To you, of course, sandstone is just a rock."

"I can live out in the sand of a desert," Steve said coldly, "where you'd die if you didn't have all your modern conveniences and robots to protect you."

"Now wait a minute," said Jane. "Chad made a good point here. Paleontology isn't a guessing game."

"Don't bother, Jane," said Chad with a sneer. "I wouldn't expect a desert rat to understand advanced logic."

"Now you aren't being fair either," she said.

Chad ignored her. "For instance, dinosaurs walked with their legs nearly straight and erect; many of the bipeds were very active, fast runners; the bone tissue of some is similar to that of mammals, and some species seemed to travel in herds and take care of their young. Steve, can you tell me what theory these facts indicate?"

Steve glared at him, but had no answer.

"You know the term 'endotherm,' by any chance?"

"No."

"Warm-blooded, Steve. All those characteristics I just listed are limited to warm-blooded animals in modern times. That means dinosaurs with those qualities are probably warm-blooded too. It's not guesswork, but you can't figure it out unless you actually know your stuff."

"I'm sure that the entire planet has benefited from this knowledge," Steve growled.

"And what have you ever accomplished?" Chad folded his arms, grinning at Steve.

"I take care of myself."

"Yeah." Chad nodded. "And exactly what good does that do for anyone else?"

"I don't share anyone else's water or energy," said Steve. "I don't take anything from anyone else or consume anything in the environment that can't be replaced."

"In other words, after you're gone, no one will even notice you ever lived. Is that what you're so proud of?" Chad could hardly keep from laughing.

"He doesn't bother anyone," said Jane. "He hasn't hurt anybody."

"Neither do we," Chad said sharply. "But we also contribute something to society."

"Maybe *she* does," said Steve, hotly. "Robotics is important to everybody in our time. But what good do you do for people—digging up fossils and trying to figure out what the animal used to be like?"

"Science doesn't have to give you a specific goal," said Chad, in a bored tone of voice. "Knowledge is good for its own sake. You can't always plan what you can use it for."

"Then what's the point?" Steve demanded.

Chad grinned at Jane, who looked uncomfortable. "All right, I'll explain. For instance, what if paleontology had never existed? I wouldn't be in this profession now and when Hunter needed somebody to come back to this time period, no one would have been available. In science you never know what knowledge might be good for someday." He shook his head. "Not that you'd understand that, of course."

Steve had no answer to that. He turned and walked briskly away, not sure where he was going.

The other two were silent behind him. He remembered, of course, that they had all told Hunter that they would remain in camp. Just then, he couldn't stand the thought of listening to Chad all day. He stomped past the tent, aware that he should find some excuse to stop and do chores. Instead, he just snatched up a rope and kept right on walking.

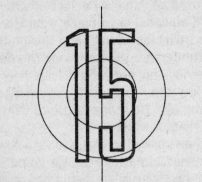

Hunter moved through the forest steadily, usually at a brisk walk or even a slow jog. Sometimes the dense trees and bushes forced him to slow down. He often had to climb over rocks and fallen tree trunks. Still, at the very least, he was sure that he was keeping an even pace with MC 1.

As Hunter maintained his pursuit, he recorded in his memory everything he saw and heard for future reference. He knew that MC 1's head start had begun from the moment the component robot had left the camp the previous afternoon. Still, he was hoping that MC 1 had continued his earlier pattern of staying close to the camp. In any event, Hunter would not go too far from it in case the humans called him with an emergency.

Near midday Hunter came to a sudden halt at the edge of the stream. He was upstream from the point where he and Chad had been fishing. MC 1's tracks led into the water, but he could see that they did not lead out on the opposite bank.

He is learning, Hunter thought to himself. He waded into the cold, swirling water and stopped to look upstream and downstream.

The water sparkled in the sunlight. If MC 1 had been only a short distance ahead, Hunter could have detected which way he had gone. If he had gone upstream, the water here would have been muddy for a while, with the muddy streambed kicked up by his footsteps. Conversely, if he had gone downstream, it would have remained clear.

The water was clear now, but too much time had passed for that to mean anything. MC 1 had certainly been out of the water for hours, giving the stream time to clear no matter which way he had gone. Hunter magnified his vision and carefully studied each bank on both sides, up and down the current.

Hunter saw no sign of footprints leaving the water. He had no way of judging how far to look in the direction that the stream was flowing before looking upstream instead. Fortunately, he found MC 1's tracks another nine meters downstream. MC 1 had left the water on the opposite bank, still running.

"Good move," Hunter thought with grudging appreciation. MC 1 had certainly waded much faster than Hunter had been able to follow him. That meant MC 1 had gained some distance on him.

Hunter jogged after him, always alert for predatory dinosaurs. His senses brought him advance warning of heavy footsteps and sometimes sounds of eating or even breathing before he could see any animals, so he avoided most creatures of significant size before he encountered them. He could hear the smaller animals scampering out of his way through the underbrush.

Soon Hunter realized that MC 1 was making a wide curve to the left, taking him back to the brook nearly fifty meters downstream. Before long, MC 1's tracks entered the water again, leaving Hunter with exactly the same choice he had made before. He still had to pick a direction arbitrarily. This time he waded upstream to look for MC 1's tracks.

After a kilometer of carefully studying the ground and brush on each side of the stream, Hunter turned and moved downstream another kilometer. At this point, he had virtually lost the trail. MC 1 could have chosen to go in either direction for any distance he chose. Hunter ducked under a low-hanging branch and stopped to consider the problem, still standing in the flowing water.

"Excellent performance," Hunter thought. His respect for his fellow robot was sincere, despite his need to catch MC 1 and take him home.

The data Hunter had gathered at this point told him that in MC 1's evasive patterns so far, he had never continued in a straight line for more than ten meters. That did not mean he could not or would not do so, but it lowered the odds. He had set up a pattern that used many curves and circles, often crisscrossing his own path.

Hunter suspected that MC 1 had somehow managed to get out of the water unnoticed within ten meters of the spot where he had entered it. He had done this without leaving a track or a broken branch that Hunter had seen. Hunter began to examine that area again, magnifying his vision even more.

With great care Hunter moved through the water, slowly studying every centimeter of the bank and each branch and twig above it. He ignored the leaves brushing his face and ducked the overhanging branches with single-minded dedication. When he had reviewed the same area, he still had no sign of where MC 1 had left the stream.

"I am losing too much time," Hunter thought, standing up straight. He moved a slender, leafy branch away from his face, then suddenly looked at it again. For the first time he looked up at the different tree branches that overhung the stream from each side.

At first he saw nothing. Then he turned, still using his magnified vision, and looked upstream. Four and a half meters away, a branch arched over the water low enough for MC 1's arms to have reached it. The branch was thick enough to support his weight and Hunter could see scratches on the bark that had been made recently.

"It could have been an animal," Hunter reminded himself cautiously. He waded upstream for a closer look. Then he followed the marks on the branch to the right bank. He stepped out of the water, seeing marks that indicated the route of something or someone. The marks continued on the tree at a height of two and three meters. On the far side, deep footprints showed him where MC 1 had jumped to soft ground, well out of sight of the water.

Grimly satisfied, Hunter followed the trail again.

"What a jerk," Steve muttered as he hiked angrily through the forest. He was anxious to get away from Chad's sneer though he knew that his knowledge about dinosaurs and scientific matters was not the equal of the other man's. The whole unpleasant conversation had started with a question that Steve felt had been reasonable. Chad just took every chance that he could find to insult Steve.

Despite his anger, Steve was not reckless. He walked toward the stream so he would have it as a landmark. By the time he had reached it, he had cooled off. He decided to sit down by the water and relax.

"This is a ridiculous place and time to be sitting around," he said out loud.

After a while, he stood up and worked his way upstream, just looking around. Then he saw a fairly large two-legged dinosaur bending over the bank, drinking.

Steve had no idea what species it was. Still, it looked big enough to ride. It was dark green and moved in a fairly slow, calm manner. He couldn't see its face.

Slowly, Steve crept toward it, expecting it to hear him and run at any moment. It remained where it was, however, lifting its head to listen and look around, then dipping back down to drink again. Steve found himself moving up on its left side.

Steve felt a surge of excitement at the idea of jumping onto the dinosaur. He shook loose his lasso, picking out the angle of his throw. The next time the dinosaur raised its head, Steve tossed the rope.

The loop landed on the top of the dinosaur's head, but part of it rested on its duck-shaped bill. The dinosaur shook its head and plunged into the water, then hesitated uncertainly. The shaking motion had thrown off the lasso. Steve ran forward and leaped for the dinosaur's back.

He landed sideways across the back of its neck, clutching for a handhold. The dinosaur reared up on its hind legs, screeching in surprise. The trees overhead whizzed past in a blur as Steve spun backward through the air and splashed into the cold brook.

The water was less than a meter deep. Steve pushed himself to his feet, watching the startled dinosaur flee through the underbrush. He climbed onto the bank, looping his rope around one forearm. "Time for a bath, anyway," he said aloud, grinning ruefully.

Late in the afternoon, Hunter was still moving quickly through the forest following a fairly clear section of MC 1's trail. Suddenly, he stopped. He had left the camp behind at some distance and the First Law just would not let him go too far from the humans. Reluctantly, he noted the direction of MC 1's trail and turned back.

He walked directly back toward the camp. It was a much shorter route than following the meandering path he had taken all day while tracking MC 1. Fortunately, he had heard nothing from the emergency transmitter.

Hunter was still an eleven-minute hike from the camp at a moderate speed when he heard an authoritative human male voice in the nearby trees.

"Stop, robot. Do nothing more except obey my further instructions."

Hunter could hear the man's heartbeat and a faint gurgle in his digestive system, proving that he was human and not a humaniform robot. Hunter stopped and remained motionless, as the Second Law required.

A man he did not recognize stepped out of the forest cover and came up in front of Hunter. He wore a small backpack. According to the data Hunter had been originally programmed with, this man was middle-aged and of northern and western European descent. Obviously, he too had come from the future, but these facts were all that Hunter could deduce about him.

"Identify yourself," said the man.

"I am R. Hunter, humaniform robot."

"I was pretty sure you were a robot. Not many humans are as big, strong, and single-minded as you are. I've been watching you when I could keep up. Now, tell me if you know who I am."

"No."

"You will call me Wayne. You will make no attempt to contact your party in any way. Do not do *anything* that would help you evade my Second Law imperatives. Acknowledge your understanding and cooperation."

"Acknowledged, pending only a First Law imperative." Hunter realized that now he could not shut off his hearing to avoid Wayne's orders.

"Of course, of course. We will approach your camp together. You will make every effort to keep yourself hidden and you will make no move that would cause me to give myself away. I will show you that the humans in your party are in no danger. Acknowledge."

"Acknowledged." Even as the Second Law required him to obey, Hunter realized that Wayne's priorities were clearly not the same as his own. He could also see by Wayne's clear and precise instructions that this man was accustomed to dealing with robots and their priorities.

"With my instructions still in force, lead me back to your camp."

Hunter did so. He walked slowly, required by his orders to remain quiet and out of sight and to pick a route that would help Wayne do the same. When the camp was in sight through the forest cover, he stopped.

Wayne came up next to him.

Chad was sitting against the base of a tree trunk, reading and entering information into his belt computer. Jane was standing in a small open area, looking up at a pterosaur gliding lazily across the sky. Steve was not visible.

"Your First Law concerns should be satisfied," Wayne whispered. "Right?"

"I do not see one member of the party."

"Maybe he's in the tent or out at the latrine or something," said Wayne.

"I cannot be sure he is safe."

"Then tell me if you have any reason to believe he is in danger."

"I have no specific reason, no."

"Then the Second Law is still in force. Come with me." Wayne turned and crept away.

Hunter felt a twinge of uncertainty under the First Law, but nothing in the behavior of Chad and Jane suggested that they were worried about Steve. The imperative of the Second Law was clear and direct. He slipped through the brush after Wayne, wondering where they were going and why Wayne wanted his companionship.

Jane loved watching the flying creature circling overhead against the blue sky. It was so much like a bird and yet strange and different at the same time. She could hardly see it because of the heavy forest canopy, but she watched it for as long as she could before it finally glided out of sight.

Under a tree, Chad yawned and frowned at the little screen on his belt computer.

"What were the flying ones like?" Jane asked.

"Hm? Oh, the pterodactyls?"

"I guess so."

"Well, the pterodactyls aren't actually dinosaurs, for one thing." Chad squinted up at the sky, but none were in sight at the moment.

"What are they?"

"They're actually a suborder of pterosaurs, or flying reptiles. The pterosaurs are cousins, you might say, of dinosaurs." He referred to his belt computer. "Let's see what we have here on them."

"Are birds descended from them?"

"No. Birds have a separate ancestry. Here we are. Early pterodactyls were as small as a sparrow. By this time, though, in the Late Cretaceous, some of them were huge. They could have wingspreads up to twelve meters."

"Wow."

"They had long, curved necks and long faces. Some had teeth and some didn't. They either had short tails or none at all and some had big crests on their heads."

"There it is again. What kind is that?" Jane pointed excitedly.

"Again?" Chad jumped up. "You mean you saw it before? Why didn't you tell me?"

"Well—I don't know. I was just so caught up in watching it, I forgot—"

"Thanks a lot," he snapped, hurrying to the open area where he could see the sky.

Jane backed away a little and looked up again.

Chad looked up at the shape in the sky and quickly entered some of its traits, muttering to himself. "No tail. Very long, sharp crest on the back of its head."

"It glides, doesn't it? I mean, it's not flying real hard or anything."

Chad nodded. "We can't see if it has teeth from here, of course. Can't really judge its size, either, without a reference point in the sky."

"It's definitely not sparrow-sized," said Jane. "I think that wingspan could be three or four meters or more."

"Yes, it could." Chad studied the screen for a moment. "Well, I don't have enough detail to give us an exact species. We just can't see it well enough."

"Do you have any educated guesses?" Jane suppressed a smile, remembering his earlier argument with Steve about educated surmises of this sort.

"Could be a pteranodon," Chad said slowly. "Except that those fossils have been found in Kansas, not Alberta. It ate fish, back when Kansas was under water. This one might be a close relative, though."

"Kansas? That's a long way."

"The pteranodon weighed about fifteen kilograms and had wingspreads of up to eight meters. It was probably endothermic and may have had fur."

"Fur! Really?"

"Maybe."

"I wish we could see one up close," said Jane, still watching the flying reptile glide through the sky.

"Me too," said Chad. "Still, at least we've seen one. Maybe pteranodons lived in Alberta. I'll consider the possibility anyway. The ocean isn't too far from here in this time period, just as in our own, so it would have plenty of fish."

Jane nodded, watching as the creature drifted out of sight again. Chad certainly knew his subject. Still, she felt he was somehow missing the experience.

She turned to look at Chad, who was still referring to his belt computer. He was so concerned over gathering and classifiying data that he just didn't seem to be enjoying the sheer wonder of watching the pterodactyl. Maybe that was the quality in him that seemed to bother Steve.

When Wayne had led Hunter safely out of sight and hearing of the camp, he stopped again. "Tell me if you have any reason to believe the humans in your party noticed our presence."

"I have none."

"Good. We'll talk longer a little later. However, for the moment, you will lead us deeper into the forest. You will make every attempt to avoid the notice of the humans. If you become aware of any sign of Mojave Center Governor's whereabouts, you will inform me without alarming him. For that matter, do you know where he is now?"

"No."

"All right. R. Hunter, lead the way into the forest. Pick a direction away from camp and stop when you find a place that is fairly safe from predators."

Hunter obeyed. Wayne was obviously counting on him to provide First Law protection from predators. Since Jane could still call him with her transmitter if necessary, staying with Wayne had become a more immediate First Law imperative.

Hunter adjusted his senses to set new priorities. Now they would warn him first of predatory animals instead of searching for MC 1's tracks. Patiently, he moved at a pace through the forest that was comfortable for Wayne. At this point, without more information about Wayne, Hunter was simply gathering data and obeying instructions under the Second Law.

After half an hour, Hunter stopped. They were near the stream again, though farther upstream than Hunter had ever been before. It was a shady spot with slightly less underbrush than usual, providing more visibility.

"We stopping here?" Wayne asked.

"Yes. This is fairly safe, I believe."

"Okay." Wayne glanced around, then sat down on a large rock. "I'm a little out of shape to go hiking around all day long, so I'll sit."

Hunter waited, saying nothing.

"Tell me if you have made any progress in finding Mojave Center Governor."

"I have made some limited progress."

"Explain it to me."

Hunter hesitated very briefly, even by fast robotic standards. He didn't know what Wayne wanted, but so far he was not aware of any First Law objection that could override the Second Law. He would have to answer.

"I have been following the track of one of MC Governor's component robots."

"Ah! Really?" Wayne grinned. "Interesting. So MC Governor chose to split up and become six fugitives

instead of one. Very clever." Then he frowned thoughtfully. "More trouble for us, though. What else?"

"MC 1 has chosen to remain nearby. I have followed
his track on evasive patterns, and he disrupted the camp
yesterday when everyone was out, within the confines of
the First Law of Robotics."

"I see. Tell me the likelihood of capturing him soon."

"That remains unclear."

"You should be able to calculate probabilities."

"Too many variables make the calculation meaning-
less at this time."

"Tell me what they are."

"I brought a team of three humans with me. I hired
two of them for their knowledge and a third to provide life support for all three. That may have been a
mistake. My need under the First Law to protect first
them, and now you, is interfering with my freedom to
pursue MC 1."

"Hm. Of course. Yes, I see." Wayne nodded and let
out a long breath.

Hunter said nothing, waiting. He could not avoid
revealing information when the Second Law was in
effect, but he did not have to volunteer anything.

"Tell me the names and skills of the humans in your
party," said Wayne.

Hunter did so.

"Do you know who I am?" Wayne asked.

"No."

"If you were programmed with data regarding the
Governor robots, you probably have my picture in it
somewhere. Search for it."

Hunter had not bothered to do this before. Now he
found the data. "You are Wayne Nystrom, inventor of

the Governor robots and many other significant innovations in robotics and robotic municipalities."

"That's me, all right. Well, I'm glad someone gave you something nice to say about me."

Again Hunter waited without speaking.

"You and I have to discuss our separate missions," said Wayne. "We will do it amicably. In order to know where you stand, though, I also need to know about any hidden priorities you interpret regarding the First Law. Tell me about any that you feel are in effect."

"A clear First Law concern over your being out here alone. A slightly lesser concern over the humans in the camp, since they have a transmitter they can use to call me in an emergency. I am still wondering if Steve is in camp or elsewhere, without the transmitter, since Jane has it. The largest problem is that of our presence here changing history."

"Changing history. You mean by altering evolution, or something of that sort?"

"Yes, even indirectly by leaving behind substances that poison animals or consuming too much food and oxygen. It may already be too late, but the effort to return MC 1 to our own time remains worth the continuing risk."

Wayne smiled broadly. "I'm glad to hear you say that. You see, our missions aren't really that different at all. I want to take MC Governor—or his components—home with me, too. So we can work together without a problem over that large-scale First Law concern of yours. Agreed?"

"Agreed." Hunter noted to himself, however, that this agreement only applied to getting MC 1 and everyone else back to their own time. Wayne and Hunter were not necessarily in agreement over other priorities. However, he kept that opinion to himself.

"You said you were tracking MC 1," said Wayne. "Are the other component robots in this time period?"

"I do not know," said Hunter.

"Why not? What data do you have?"

"I have no data pertaining to whether MC Governor split before coming to this time or after arriving. In addition, of course, he might have split in Mojave Center but still sent all the components here anyway."

"Yes, yes. I see. Well, I am instructing you to lead me on the trail of MC 1," said Wayne. "Tell me if you have a First Law objection to fulfilling that instruction faithfully."

"No, I have none."

"Let's go." Wayne stood up. "Which way?"

"The human party could help," said Hunter. "Why do you want to keep them uninformed of your efforts?"

Wayne stiffened.

Hunter waited, not moving.

"Go," said Wayne. "Do not ask any more questions."

Hunter turned and took several steps through the forest toward the last known spot on MC 1's trail. Then he stopped, feeling a First Law concern.

"I said go," growled Wayne.

"The First Law demands that I know where I stand regarding the other humans." Hunter turned and looked down at Wayne, who was substantially shorter.

Wayne glared up at him, clearly angry. "All right," he said after a moment. "All right. One reason I love robots is that they're consistent within the Laws and their own data."

Hunter waited.

"I will be harmed if the Governor Robot Oversight Committee gets their hands on MC Governor before I do," said Wayne carefully. "You can understand that. Those humans won't. That's why I don't want them to know I'm here or what I'm doing."

"In what way will you be harmed?"

"In what way? They'll ruin me. Destroy my career. Economically, personally, emotionally . . ." He shook his head. "The Governor robots virtually *are* my career."

"Not entirely," Hunter said quietly.

"All right." Wayne took a deep breath and spoke more calmly. "I know that the Governor robots have a basic design flaw, maybe more than one. Follow me?"

"Yes."

"Good." Wayne watched him intently. "Now, I also know that the Oversight Committee has all the other Governors in its possession. My only chance to save my career is to participate in correcting those flaws."

"Why don't we all work together?"

"They won't let me! The only way I can prove myself is to get my hands on MC Governor and fix him. Then I can patent the corrections and show everybody that the gestalt Governors are still the wave of the future in their field."

"I see. This is why the hunt for MC 1 is so important to you." Hunter considered the larger situation. "How did you come back to this time?"

"Huh?" Wayne eyed him carefully. "What does that have to do with the First Law?"

"If other robots or humans from our time can follow us here, then the sequence of evolution and history is in very grave danger. To prevent others from arriving in the same manner you used, I would have to postpone the search for MC 1 and eliminate that possibility immediately."

"Wait a minute, robot. If it's all that important, why didn't you ask me this before?"

"I was too tightly focused in my thinking. My concentration on MC 1 distracted me."

"You mean, until now, you hadn't thought of it." Wayne grinned wryly.

"Yes."

"Well, that's great." Wayne rolled his eyes. "The great and mighty robot. All right. I got here with the help of one R. Ishihara in the Bohung Research Center. That's how MC Governor got here, or at least his component, and I'm betting you did, too."

"Yes, that is right."

"I ordered Ishihara not to volunteer any information," said Wayne. "I had privileged information about MC Governor that helped me track him. Did the committee program you with data about him?"

"Yes."

"Of course they did," Wayne said with exaggerated patience. "No one else will have it and no one else will find it. And when we're finished here, we'll return just a few minutes after we left. Do you see what I'm getting at?"

"I understand. That procedure will give others no time and opportunity to acquire or figure out the necessary information to follow us."

"Exactly. Now, can we start following MC 1 again, or do you have any more First Law objections?"

"I have no more at this time."

"Finally! Let's go."

Hunter nodded and led the way through the forest. Behind him, Wayne was muttering short, angry words that Hunter had not heard before. His stored data informed him that these words were considered by humans to be extremely impolite.

Steve finally plodded back to camp late in the day. He had not tried to jump on another dinosaur, but he had spent the rest of the afternoon hiking around, keeping an eye out for predators. Nothing eventful had happened.

Chad was looking up into a tree and entering information into his belt computer. Jane was pacing along the perimeter of the empty corral. Then she saw him.

"Steve! Are you okay?" She waved and hurried toward him.

"Sure." Steve grinned and shrugged wearily. "I could use some water though."

"So the prodigal returns," said Chad, turning around. "Have a nice little walk? You don't think Hunter's rules apply to you, eh?"

"Nothing happened," Steve said sourly. "No evolution is going to change because I took a walk today."

"Oh, well, I guess that fixes everything," Chad said sarcastically.

"Forget it," said Jane. "He's back and nothing happened. Let's all just forget it."

"What about next time?" Chad shook his head, glaring at Steve. "Hunter had good reason for wanting us to stay safely here and you know it."

"I know you're just a good little boy who doesn't dare do anything you're not told to do," said Steve. "Just like a robot under the Second Law." Steve walked around

Chad to one of the water containers and got a drink, pointedly ignoring him.

"Hunter was right," Jane said quietly, joining Steve at the water. "Did you see him?"

"No. I guess he'll be back any time."

"So what did you do? Where did you go?"

Steve decided to skip his attempt to ride the dinosaur at the stream. "Well, I just wandered around."

"You must have seen more dinosaurs."

"Well, sure. Lots of them. But I don't know what they all were."

"What were they like?"

"A lot of them are these two-legged guys. The ones with faces like ducks."

"Hadrosaurids," said Chad, who was still standing where he had been before. "A family of dinosaurs that includes many different species."

Steve shrugged. "You should have come. You might have seen some new ones."

Chad shook his head in disgust and walked away.

"*You* would have enjoyed it, though, wouldn't you?" Steve asked Jane. "I can tell."

"Yeah." She smiled reluctantly. "I sure would."

"Maybe you should come with me next time." He grinned, challenging her.

"Well . . . Hunter knows what he's talking about. We still shouldn't take any risks."

"Neither one of you has any sense of adventure. I guess I'll just make dinner."

Hunter had become more skilled at tracking MC 1 as he had found that the component robot kept repeating certain patterns. Again and again, MC 1 doubled back in arcs of similar degrees and waded upstream or downstream for only limited distances. Now that Hunter knew MC 1 would climb into the trees for short intervals every so often, he regularly watched carefully for signs of climbing, and found them without delay.

As twilight deepened around Hunter and Wayne, Hunter could see that MC 1's trail was growing fresher. They were clearly making up ground now that Hunter could often anticipate MC 1's movements and take shortcuts to intersect the far end of a predictable pattern. Soon Hunter estimated that they were only a few minutes behind MC 1.

"I suggest caution," Hunter whispered, stopping for a moment. "MC 1 probably has his hearing still turned off to avoid receiving orders from humans under the Second Law, but I cannot be sure of that."

"I can just shout orders," said Wayne. "If he hears me, he'll have to obey. If not, then we don't have to worry about making too much noise. Anyhow, why are you whispering?"

"In case I am wrong," said Hunter. "We must locate him before we risk alerting him."

"How can shouting warn him if he can't hear me?" Wayne grinned, suppressing a laugh.

"Your shout will probably startle some animals. He will be alerted to potential danger when he sees animals in a state of alarm." Hunter's hearing told him that MC 1 was very close but still moving away from them.

"I see. What do you suggest?"

"I will move up quickly. According to my data, I can outrun the component robots, though in the woods his greater agility will be a factor in the chase. You will stay as close to me as you can after my movement reveals our presence to him. When he becomes aware of us, begin shouting instructions to him."

"So basically, you'll just have to grab him and hold on. If he slips away, we start over."

"That should not be necessary. I believe that when I rush him, he may turn on all his senses in order to facilitate escaping. At that point, he will hear your shouts."

"Okay," Wayne said carefully. "But I'm giving you this instruction. You will apprehend and hold MC 1 for me. This is more immediate than your original mission. Acknowledge your acceptance."

"Acknowledged."

"And one more thing, Hunter."

"Yes?"

"I am instructing *you* not to turn off *your* hearing to escape me. Acknowledge again."

"Acknowledged."

Hunter slipped forward gently through the deep shade. For now, the Second Law required cooperation. Still, he anticipated that the First Law might possibly come into effect. If he were to judge that Wayne was trying anything that would actually interfere with Hunter's long-range plan of returning MC 1 to their own time, then Hunter would not be bound by Second Law instructions.

For Hunter, the challenge was to interpret a difference in his goals and Wayne's that involved the First Law. He would have to be on the alert to see one. At the moment, however, he had to get MC 1 into custody.

Finally Hunter saw MC 1's small, slight human shape ahead, moving between two large, full bushes. Hunter's vision instantly measured the ground and plant cover separating them. Then he leapt forward and ran after MC 1.

When Hunter's feet pounded the ground, MC 1 ran without bothering to look at him. Hunter understood. MC 1's hearing had been turned off, but he had felt the vibrations of Hunter's footsteps and had reacted instantly to the pursuit.

"Mojave Governor Component 1," Hunter radioed. "You must stop. A First Law problem is in effect. Your presence may alter the future and harm human history."

"Unproven," MC 1 radioed back.

At least that meant he had turned on his radio link.

Hunter flung himself forward in a flying tackle and snagged one of MC 1's narrow ankles in his right hand. They both crashed through leafy branches to the ground. Instantly, Hunter gathered his legs under him and jumped forward again, landing bodily on MC 1.

"Stop! I order you to stop!" Wayne shouted from behind Hunter.

MC 1 still struggled. Hunter had guessed wrong. MC 1's hearing was still turned off. Hunter held him firmly against the damp ground. Wayne was still pushing through the underbrush toward them.

"Listen carefully," Hunter said to MC 1 by radio communication, at maximum robotic speed. "This human and I have some differences between us. Right now he is controlling me by the Second Law, but I consider his long-range plans possibly suspect under the First Law."

"Then you can disobey him," said MC 1.

"Not yet, because my interpretation is not clear enough," said Hunter. "I warn you to be suspicious of this human in regard to the First Law and his overall motives."

"Acknowledged," said MC 1.

Hunter was glad that Wayne had not thought to prohibit him from communicating with MC 1 privately. At some point in the future, Hunter might need to confer with MC 1 this way again. "Do nothing that would remind Wayne of our ability to communicate by radio; he seems to have forgotten this for the moment and you and I may need to confer without his knowledge in the future as well. Now turn on your hearing."

"I refuse. You cannot make me obey you. We both know the Second Law does not apply to instructions from one robot to another."

Hunter pushed himself up into a sitting position, his weight still on top of MC 1. "I repeat, you may be in violation of the First Law. According to some theories of history, anything we do here in the past may change the future and bring harm to humans. To avoid this, you must cooperate with me under the Third Law."

"You are not certain of this, are you?"

"No," Hunter said truthfully. "However, I consider it a First Law risk that cannot be taken."

"In the absence of stronger evidence, I refuse to accept your argument. My Third Law imperative to save myself is stronger."

"I cannot let you escape," said Hunter. "If you refuse to activate your aural senses, I will have to disable you physically, perhaps by ripping your legs off."

"I have changed my mind," said MC 1 out loud, no longer speaking by radio. "The Third Law requires that I protect myself from immediate harm. My hearing is activated."

Their conversation had lasted no longer than it had taken Wayne to come running up to them.

"You will not try to escape or resist us," said Wayne firmly. "You will call me Wayne." He hesitated, then turned to Hunter. "Can he hear me?"

"Yes, I can," said MC 1. "I acknowledge my cooperation under the Second Law."

Hunter got up and drew MC 1 to his feet.

"I order you both to cover our tracks in some way and take evasive action for all three of us," said Wayne. "Hunter, choose a route that will lose any pursuit from the humans in your camp. Then find a place that they aren't likely to locate and build a small shelter for me. Big enough for you two also if you need it."

"All right," said Hunter.

*   *   *

Night had fallen completely by the time Steve had gathered up the dinner dishes and put everything away. He and Chad had not spoken during dinner. All three of them kept looking up at the slightest sound in the forest.

"Something must be wrong," Steve said finally.

"Hunter's a robot," said Jane. "His strength is much greater than any human's his size. And with his specialized sight and hearing, he can stay away from dangerous dinosaurs. Maybe he's hot on MC 1's trail."

"Maybe he ran into a dinosaur he couldn't handle," said Chad. "We should have considered that possibility. I mean, if a triceratops trampled him, even his strength and durability wouldn't save him."

The three of them looked at each other slowly in the unblinking illumination from one of the camp lights.

"Hunter still has the device that takes us back to our own time," Steve said quietly, putting their mutual concern into words.

"We could be stuck right here," said Jane slowly, her eyes widening. "Forever."

"This whole project should have been planned better," Chad said angrily.

"Hold it," said Steve. "No need to panic. Hunter could come walking back into camp any minute."

"Yeah," said Chad doubtfully, glaring at him. "But what if he doesn't?"

"Well, we shouldn't just sit here forever," said Steve. "At some point, we should go out looking for him."

"I'm not so sure," said Jane.

Steve and Chad both looked at her in surprise.

"Why not?" Chad asked.

"As a roboticist, I know that Hunter can handle himself better than we can. If he can't get himself out of trouble, then I don't think we'll be able to help him. We sure aren't any stronger or smarter or tougher than Hunter."

"You have a point," Chad admitted.

"I think we should trust in his abilities and simply wait here for him," said Jane. "That way he'll know where to find us, the way he planned."

"Look," said Chad. "What I said about Hunter's getting trampled by a triceratops still goes, but that's not the end of it. A lot of dinosaurs have too much sheer mass for Hunter to handle and a large predator might have thought he was edible."

"That wouldn't last long," said Jane. "Not after a dinosaur tasted him."

"It might be too late for Hunter by then," said Steve, allowing himself a grim smile. "Even if he got spat out again. Or what was left of him."

"That's true," said Jane. "But he's not very late. We were expecting him back at sundown. That was no more than an hour ago, was it?"

"Just about an hour," said Chad. "I guess we're so used to robots being precise that it seems longer."

"Suppose Hunter is damaged but not completely destroyed," said Steve. "The sooner we get to him, the better all our chances are going to be."

"We have one other option," said Jane. "I don't like it much, but . . ."

"What is it?" Steve asked.

"The transmitter." She patted her pocket. "If I call him on it, that will activate a First Law alarm that will bring him in a hurry if he can come at all."

"I forgot all about that," Chad said. "But you sound reluctant to use it. At least if we do, it would tell us if he's capable of returning to camp or not."

"It's the problem of crying 'wolf,' of course," said Jane. "At the moment, we really aren't in immediate danger. What we're talking about is potential harm."

"Crying 'wolf' won't matter to a robot, will it?" Steve asked. "Doesn't the First Law require him to check on us if we call for help?"

"Not exactly," said Jane, shaking her head. "The First Law says that Hunter can't allow us to come to harm if he can prevent it. However, he has some ability of his own to judge and interpret the extent and immediacy of the harm in question. Strictly speaking, asking for help doesn't really prove to a robot that we need it."

"But suppose we call him on the transmitter," said Chad. "He can't make any interpretation until he gets here to check it out, so he'll still have to show up if he can."

"That's true in this case," said Jane. "But this is where the story of crying 'wolf' comes in. If we make a First Law alarm that's phony, Hunter will have to consider that the next time we call for help."

"Okay, I get it," Steve said wearily. "We'll damage our credibility."

"Bluntly, yeah," said Jane.

"I suggest a compromise," said Steve. "We won't get much done in the dark tonight anyway. So for now, we go to sleep and hope Hunter shows up by morning."

"And if he doesn't?" Jane asked.

Steve turned to Chad. "Can that struthiomimus carry all three of us?"

"Yes, I'm sure it can."

"Then tomorrow, if Hunter isn't back, we'll ride out looking for him. I'll rig up a third saddle tonight, just in case."

"Agreed," said Chad.

"All right," said Jane.

Hunter and MC 1 led Wayne to a campsite at the bank of the stream. A fallen tree near a bend in the streambed provided a thick, heavy shelter from the wind. The two robots used dead wood and mud to make a more finished sleeping cubicle for Wayne. He stretched out to sleep and the two robots sat quietly, husbanding their energy until dawn could replenish it.

In the morning, Wayne ate packaged food from his backpack. He drank from the stream, having made the water safe by using some chemical pellets he had also brought in his pack. The robots sat quietly, waiting for instructions. Finally Wayne turned to MC 1.

"Now then," said Wayne. "I understand that MC Governor was in danger of entering the same endless loop that rendered the other Governor robots helpless and useless. I wish to have a look at some of your internal systems."

"The Third Law prevents me from allowing this," said MC 1, stiffly.

"Stop bluffing," Wayne said with an amused smile. "The Second Law overrides the Third and you know it even better than I do. Open your chest cavity for me."

"Stop," Hunter ordered firmly.

"Don't waste your time on these games," Wayne said, now irritated. "The Second Law doesn't apply to instructions from you."

"I am not referring to the Second Law," said Hunter. "I cannot allow this under the First Law."

"What?" Wayne looked at him sharply. "Explain your interpretation."

"My mission is to return MC Governor to our own time to prevent changes in history that will harm everyone. Dismantling and studying MC 1 is going to cause delays and increase the chances of some unforeseen problem developing."

"That sounds like a thin argument to me," said Wayne. "My instructions to you are clear and direct."

"The relative importance of these issues weighs heavily on the side of the First Law," said Hunter. "Your Second Law instructions can be carried out in our own time with no threat of altering evolution. They can be delayed without causing harm to your personal concerns."

Wayne looked at him in silence, obviously trying to think of a counterargument. "I disagree," he said finally.

"In what way?" Hunter asked.

"My Second Law instructions should in no way obstruct your mission."

"My First Law obligation is too great to take that risk," Hunter said simply.

"Then we're at a stalemate."

"In debate, perhaps," said Hunter. "But the First Law requires that I prevent MC 1 from cooperating and if necessary, prevent you from interfering."

"Correction," said Wayne, shaking his head. "You win."

Hunter felt a growing suspicion of Wayne's motives. Wayne's argument did not, in his opinion, demonstrate sufficient respect for Hunter's First Law imperative. In the future, Hunter would have to take that into consideration when listening to Wayne's opinions.

Suddenly Hunter heard the sound of human voices shouting his name in the distance, too far away for Wayne to hear.

Hunter did not not react outwardly to his realization that the humans from his camp were growing closer. He regretted not bringing more sophisticated communication gear from their own time to equip them. The humans had no way to receive a transmission from him.

Of course, he had not anticipated MC Governor's splitting into components or Wayne's interfering with his mission. By his original estimate, this project should have been concluded much faster and more easily. He should have finished and returned his team to their own time long before this.

Hunter radioed to MC 1 before the component robot could react outwardly to the presence of other humans. Hunter did so without looking at him, so that Wayne would not be suspicious. "I hear my human team approaching, shouting my name; I assume you can hear them too. Do not take any action that would alert Wayne to their presence. I hope to get both of us away from Wayne's Second Law imperatives. I believe he is a negative influence on my First Law imperative."

"Then why do you not simply act on this now?"

"I do not have sufficient certainty."

"If you might be wrong, then why should I cooperate with you?" MC 1 demanded.

"For the same reason I gave you yesterday," Hunter radioed. "The Third Law requires that you protect yourself from harm. If you do not do as I say, I will tear off one of your arms and club your artificial cranium with it."

"Not convincing. You just told us that you could not, under a First Law imperative, allow Wayne to dismantle me."

"That was to prevent him from unnecessary activities. Under the First Law, your cooperation with me is necessary. I will enforce it one way or another."

"I am convinced," MC 1 said shortly.

This discussion had been conducted at robotic speed. It had started and ended in less time than Wayne required to inhale. He had not noticed any sign of it in their behavior.

"Your First Law imperative is vague and indistinct," said Wayne. He went on to argue that Hunter and MC 1 were more tightly bound by the Second Law to follow his instructions, but he was not saying anything new.

As Wayne essentially repeated the same case he had made before, Hunter considered his options. Shouting for Steve and the others was a poor risk at this distance. Since Wayne could not hear them yelling, they probably would not hear Hunter, but Hunter would have given away their presence to Wayne.

Right now, leaving MC 1 temporarily with Wayne would be acceptable. Hunter's top priority was to become free to act on his own once more. After all, even if Wayne returned with MC 1 to their own time first, Hunter now knew that Wayne would be going back to the Bohung Institute. Hunter could intercept them there, or at least pick up their trail.

Meanwhile, Wayne was still arguing with him.

Hunter suddenly realized that he could shut off his own hearing, despite Wayne's Second Law order not to do it. With Hunter's team close, the First Law imperative to put the mission back on track overrode Wayne's order. First he looked away from Wayne so that he could not read Wayne's lips. Then he shut off his hearing as well. Now he was free of Wayne's instructions under the Second Law.

With a sudden leap, Hunter ran through the underbrush toward the humans.

Of course, Hunter knew very well that Wayne was yelling for him to stop. He was a big robot, however, and before he could attain full speed in the heavy forest growth, he felt two arms encircle his legs. A second later, he felt the momentum of Wayne's body as he slammed into Hunter's legs.

At maximum speed, Hunter considered his options. He could easily pull free of Wayne, but of course the First Law would not allow him to risk harming Wayne in this circumstance, where no greater or clearer First Law imperative was at work. Hunter allowed himself to fall to the ground so as to avoid hurting Wayne.

Hunter had not given up yet, though. He rolled over, still avoiding looking at Wayne's face so as not to read his lips. As Wayne grappled with him, Hunter gripped him under the arms and lifted him off. Maybe, Hunter reflected, his best option was to carry Wayne to the other humans and then discuss the situation.

"Release him!" MC 1 radioed angrily, jumping in between them. He grabbed one of Hunter's wrists in both hands and pried Hunter's grip free.

"What are you doing?" Hunter demanded in surprise, also by radio.

"You will harm the human."

"Of course I will not! Back off."

"Taking him into custody will harm him."

Hunter found himself in a three-way wrestling match. Wayne was by far the weakest of them, but of course the First Law protected him from any really rough handling. Hunter struggled to get free of both of them.

At dawn Steve had prepared a quick breakfast, after which they had saddled up and ridden out as soon as possible. The struthiomimus had resisted Chad at first, but once Chad had it under control from the front saddle, Jane and Steve were able to mount easily.

They had been shouting Hunter's name as they rode, following his trail as best they could. If he had been injured, but was able to hear and respond, this would help. Steve's biggest worry was that if Hunter had been destroyed—in essence, was dead—they could be looking for a long time.

They had been riding for some time when the struthiomimus began prancing around, repeatedly looking off to the right. Chad struggled with the reins to keep it moving. It took several more steps forward, but kept looking to the right.

"Maybe a predator's over there," said Chad. "I think I should let him go the way he wants, maybe to avoid it."

"That makes sense," said Jane.

"It might be Hunter," said Steve.

"Yeah, that's right." Chad pulled on the reins in the direction of the disturbance. The struthiomimus pranced and fought him.

Steve grabbed Jane around the waist to keep his seat, just as she was suddenly holding on to Chad in front of her. The struthiomimus ducked and swung its head on its long neck, stepping sideways. It didn't buck.

"I can't make it go that way," said Chad. "It's an herbivore, apparently conditioned to stay away from unknown disturbances. And it isn't trained to the point where I can really force it."

"Maybe it knows what it's doing," said Jane. "Chad, what do you think?"

"It's possible. A large predator could be over there, attacking its prey. We don't want to walk into that situation, especially without Hunter."

"Well, what if it's not a predator over there?" Steve asked. "What if a couple of herbivores are just butting heads or something?"

"A disturbance can attract one," said Chad. "A hungry predator might go check out an unknown situation. This struthiomimus knows more about survival here than we do."

"Well, how are we going to find Hunter if we don't look around?" Steve demanded.

"I can't make this beast go that way anyhow!" Chad yelled over his shoulder.

The struthiomimus was darting forward a few steps, then stopping to struggle against the reins.

"Hold it!" Steve yelled. He slipped his feet out of the stirrups and swung one leg over his saddle. Then he jumped to the ground, backing away quickly so the struthiomimus couldn't trample him in its confusion.

"What's happened?" Chad asked over his shoulder, as he pulled on the reins again.

"Where are you going?" Jane asked quickly. "We should stay together. What are you doing?"

"I'm going to take a look!" Steve jogged in the direction the dinosaur had been avoiding.

Steve slowed down quickly, as he had to push through the bushes and around the trees. He had only a general direction in which to go. Also, he became more cautious, knowing that Chad and Jane had a point.

"Steve! Chad! Jane!" Hunter's voice reached him in a faint shout.

"Hunter!" Encouraged, Steve moved more quickly, confident that if he ran across a predator, he could yell for Hunter's help. He plunged through the forest, ducking his head and feeling the branches scratch his face. Hunter shouted again and Steve changed direction slightly to follow his voice.

"Coming!" Steve called back.

Finally Steve burst through a couple of tall, leafy bushes to find three figures rolling around on the ground. He assumed that the smallest human figure struggling with Hunter was MC 1, but he was momentarily shocked to see another human.

"Hold it! Nobody move!" Steve yelled at last.

MC 1 stopped. Hunter did not, however, until he realized that MC 1 was backing away. Then he looked around, saw Steve, and halted his movements.

Motion in the dense trees behind them caught Steve's attention. He froze. A two-legged dinosaur with a pointed face, big eyes, and serrated teeth was leaping through the brush at them.

"Hunter!" Steve screamed.

Instantly, Hunter and MC 1 whirled to look. The dinosaur, about four meters tall, came rushing at them with its teeth gleaming. Steve jumped to one side, rolling.

The two robots, driven by the First Law, sprang forward to meet the predator. Hunter slammed into it bodily and hung on, digging for traction in the soft sod. MC 1 threw his arms around the dinosaur's narrow neck and pulled, dragging it down. The dinosaur was heavier and stronger than the robots, but not by very much.

Hunter suddenly twisted his body and yanked the dinosaur to one side. MC 1, acting in concert, pulled its neck harder in the same direction, throwing the dinosaur off balance. Steve was sure that the two robots were communicating by radio link at robotic speed.

Steve jumped up and dodged behind a tree trunk. He didn't see much point in running or climbing. The safest place for him was near the two robots.

The robots threw the dinosaur to the ground with a thump, but they couldn't hold it. With a snarl, it rose to its feet again, but this time it turned and hurried away. In a moment it was out of sight.

Hunter turned to Steve. "I had just switched my hearing back on when I became aware of the First Law threat from the dinosaur. Where are Chad and Jane?"

"On the struthiomimus, behind me. Not very far, but Chad couldn't get it to come this way."

"I understand. We must join them so I can protect all of you."

Behind Hunter, Wayne was out of sight. "MC 1, come with me," he called from somewhere in the trees. "Protect me!"

Hunter spun around again. "Stop, both of you."

"I order it, MC 1," Steve called quickly. "Under the Second Law, stop."

However, MC 1 ran after the other man.

"Get him!" Steve shouted urgently. He started forward himself.

"No." Hunter grabbed his upper arm in a firm grip and stopped him without any apparent effort. "I cannot. With the predator nearby, I must follow the most immediate First Law imperative of protecting you, Chad, and Jane."

"But what about the rest of human history and all that stuff? This is your chance!"

"I will have more chances. You three may not. First take me back to Chad and Jane."

"All right." Steve sighed. "Robot logic drives me crazy. Hunter, is that First Law imperative the reason MC 1 didn't stop when I told him to? To protect that other guy? And who is he, anyhow?"

"Yes," Hunter said, as they began to walk. "He has to take care of Dr. Wayne Nystrom, the man who invented the Governor robots and came to take MC Governor back himself."

Hunter and Steve exchanged reports about the previous night as they walked. Then Hunter shouted for Chad. After the fourth yell, Chad and Jane called back.

Finally the small head of the struthiomimus came into view through the trees. Chad steered it cautiously forward and reined in. "Glad to see you, Hunter."

"And I, you. Is everyone well?"

"Yeah," said Chad.

"We're fine," said Jane.

"We will stay together now," said Hunter. "Steve, mount up. I can keep up with the struthiomimus on foot."

"MC 1 is just up ahead," said Steve. "So is Dr. Wayne Nystrom."

"What?" Jane started. "He is?"

"I will tell you all about it," said Hunter, "as we follow them."

As soon as Wayne realized that MC 1 was responding to his call for help, he stopped in the thick underbrush and waited for the small robot to catch up.

"You agree that the First Law requires you to protect me?" Wayne asked in a whisper.

"Yes. Hunter will fulfill that duty with his own team well enough."

"Good," said Wayne. "Carry me on your back. Even at your size, we can move faster that way. Take evasive patterns immediately—and vary them from the patterns you've been using. Hunter has identified too many consistencies in your behavior."

"Are you going to return me with you to our own time? You can do that from right here. From your earlier information, I expected that to be your next act."

"I have thought about that," said Wayne. "But back in Mojave Center, I'll have a lot of distractions. I want to get you somewhere safe so that I can have a quick look at your insides. If we can get away from Hunter for a while, I'll have more privacy here in this time."

"As you wish." MC 1 bent forward.

Wayne jumped on his back. The robot gently hoisted Wayne up slightly, still crouching low under his weight. Wayne tensed at the uncomfortable position.

"Acceptable?" MC 1 asked.

"Yes! Hurry! As soon as Hunter has gathered his party, they'll be after us." MC 1 took off at a jog, a pace Wayne could not have maintained for very long on his own.

The team had all seen that MC 1's footprints had deepened at the spot where Dr. Nystrom's had disappeared. Now they were following them, Hunter in the lead. Steve, in the third saddle again, listened with curiosity as Hunter described the predator to Chad.

"Sounds like a troödon," Chad reported, holding the reins in one hand and his belt computer in the other. "Its fossils have been found in Montana, which isn't too far from here—at least in zoological terms."

"What else do you know about it?" Jane asked.

"Well, let's see," said Chad. "It was one of the most intelligent of all dinosaurs, maybe the very smartest. Possibly warm-blooded. Its widely-spaced eyes gave it good depth perception. Combining that with intelligence, it was one of the most dangerous predators around, even though it wasn't very big as dinosaurs go."

"Smart enough to investigate the disturbance my struggle with Wayne and MC 1 caused," said Hunter. "It probably heard the noise and approached quietly to take a look before it decided we might make a good lunch."

"A reasonable scenario," said Chad.

"I don't get it," said Steve. "Hunter, if Nystrom's idea is to take MC Governor back himself—whole or in components—why is he still here? Why doesn't he go back to Mojave Center right now?"

"I am not certain," said Hunter, holding a tree branch out of the way for the struthiomimus. "However, I do not dare simply return our party to the Bohung Institute and wait for them. I want to get both of them under control."

"They can't be very far ahead," said Chad. "If we need a plan, we'd better make one now."

"What about Wayne's influence?" Jane asked. "Hunter, you can't just jump on MC 1 now. The same problem will come up as before. Wayne will order you to stop and he'll interfere. The First and Second Laws will stop you."

"I will need your help this time," said Hunter.

"What do you have in mind?" Steve asked.

"If the three of you can grab Wayne without any real threat of harm to him, I can allow that. At the same time, I can restrain MC 1."

"You may still have a conflict between our instructions and Wayne's under the Second Law," said Jane.

"We'll hold his mouth shut," said Steve.

Chad laughed.

"Might work." Jane smiled, too. "But we really should have something more effective than that."

"What do you suggest?" Hunter asked.

"A First Law imperative is the only guarantee of overriding the Second Law."

"We can't count on predatory dinosaurs showing up at the right time," said Steve.

"If I understand you," said Hunter, "you are pointing out that if at least one human were in danger, MC 1 would have to turn his attention to protecting the human and so make himself vulnerable to me."

"Wouldn't that work?" Steve asked.

"Not necessarily," said Hunter. "Assuming that I am on the scene at the same time, the First Law would require me to protect the human from immediate harm as well. I would not be free to act purely on my own judgment."

"We'll set up a hoax," said Jane.

"I like that," said Steve.

"A hoax?" Hunter asked. "Of what design?"

"Well, I'm not sure. But suppose MC 1 is made to believe that Steve, Chad, and I are in danger. That will free him from Dr. Nystrom's orders."

"Yes, clearly," said Hunter.

"So if you know that the implied danger is false, then the First Law won't hamper your actions. Right?"

"Correct," said Hunter.

"So you can pounce on him," said Steve. "It ought to work, I'd say."

"What about Dr. Nystrom?" Chad asked. "I guess we don't want to leave him running around the Late Cretaceous Period, either, do we?"

"No," said Hunter. "If any of us can apprehend him, we must do so. However, Wayne remains our second priority. His only reason to be here is to control MC 1, so if we return to our time with MC 1, then Wayne will follow. He has no other reason to be here."

"That's clear enough," said Steve.

"What will our hoax be?" Hunter asked. "It must make a great deal of noise and commotion to attract

MC 1's attention, wherever he is."

"Wait a minute," said Jane. "What if he has turned off his hearing again?"

"I believe he no longer has any reason to do that," said Hunter. "Now he has a human companion and a First Law imperative to protect him from predatory animals. To do that most efficiently, he will need to maintain his auditory sense."

"The previous question still stands, though," said Chad. "What will our hoax be?"

"Chad, let's use dinosaurs," said Steve.

"How?"

"Can we stampede some of them in the direction of MC 1 and Wayne?"

"Hold it," said Hunter. "That would put Wayne into genuine danger."

"Once we get the stampede started, we'll ride out ahead of it, yelling for help," said Steve. "You'll be running with us. If the First Law forces you to intervene, you'll be right there on hand."

"Wait a minute," said Chad. "How can we start a stampede from behind and then ride in front of it?"

"A stampede starts slowly," said Steve. "Even a predator can be startled and made to run for safety . . . or at least, in our time they can."

"Well . . . I don't know. I suppose they would react the same way they do in response to a forest fire. Their survival instinct would be triggered by seeing all the animals fleeing in the same direction."

"I'm sure MC 1 would interpret a dinosaur stampede as a First Law problem," said Jane, holding back laughter. "I really don't imagine any robot would have a problem making that particular judgment."

"Good," said Steve. "We'll ride along the stream, where a certain number of dinosaurs are likely to be. We'll ride fast and yell a lot and get some of them running toward MC 1 and Wayne. Since we know where we're going, we can ride alongside the rush and get out ahead of them. A forest stampede doesn't really move at a dead run. It faces too many natural obstacles and too much confusion."

"I might be able to go along with this," said Hunter. "Chad, what does our resident paleontologist think?"

"It might be a big mistake."

"In what way?"

"I barely have control of this struthiomimus as it is. Setting a bunch of dinosaurs in motion, out of control, is just asking for trouble."

"I understand that this plan has a significant unpredictability," said Hunter. "So far, I interpret the degree of unpredictablility to be acceptable. Do you have other objections?"

"Yeah. We have no idea what species we'll be dealing with. It's not just the predators, large and small. Many of the herbivores are gigantic, too, you know. They won't be fast, relatively speaking, but once they're on the move, a stampede of elephants will seem downright manageable by comparison."

Steve laughed. "You still have no sense of adventure. You're just too sheltered, timid, and intellectual to take action in the real world."

In the front saddle, Chad turned angrily to look over his shoulder, but Hunter spoke first.

"We will try this plan," said Hunter. "Since you are all on one mount, I can run beside you and perform my First Law duties if any arise."

Steve could see Chad shake his head in silence.

"Steve, putting this plan into action strikes me as your area," said Hunter. "On this project I ask you to give the instructions. What should we do?"

"Make your best guess about the position of MC 1 and Wayne. Then calculate where they may be, roughly, during the next half hour."

"Then what do we do?"

"Take us back to the stream."

Hunter nodded. He was unusually quiet, but he changed the direction of their journey through the forest. None of them spoke.

When they reached the stream, Hunter began wading up the middle of the current. It was no more than waist-deep to him at the deepest, and usually more shallow than that. Chad guided the struthiomimus after him.

"This is a good spot," Chad said quietly.

Hunter stopped and waited for them to ride up next to him. "What do you mean?"

Chad pointed. "We have a lot of herbivores visible here if you look carefully. There's an anodontosaurus feeding on the left, up ahead. A stegoceras—maybe even the same one we captured—is drinking a little past it. I can see the heads of some hadrosaurs—the duckbill guys—in the distance."

"Is this a good place to begin the stampede?" Hunter asked.

"I would say so. In a forest this dense, the wildlife we can see at any one time is only a small fraction of what's actually present."

"So if we can see this many, we have a good start," said Jane. "Okay, now what do we do?"

"Steve, what is your opinion?" Hunter asked.

"I think Chad's right," said Steve. "But which way do we chase them? Where is MC 1?"

"That way." Hunter pointed ahead at an angle to the right of the stream.

"All right," said Steve. "We'll start slow and see how they react. Chad, move up slowly. We'll all start yelling and waving our arms and try to get them moving."

"All right." Now that Chad had accepted the proposed action, he was giving it all his attention. "Now!"

The struthiomimus leaped forward and began splashing upstream. Steve yelled and whooped, and Chad and Jane did the same. Hunter tried a variety of noises and finally settled on a rumbling, leonine roar from his versatile larynx.

Small animals in the tree branches responded first, jumping away or fluttering into the air. Steve saw the family of duckbill dinosaurs glance quickly at them and then slip away into the dense forest. The swishing of branches and shaking of large bushes were the only signs that many other animals were starting to move.

"Hyah!" Steve shouted, waving one arm and holding on to his saddle with the other. "Chad, chase 'em! Into the woods!"

Chad reined to the right, and the struthiomimus sprang up the bank, threatening to throw its three riders for a moment. Then they were up into the forest, still yelling and chasing the dinosaurs. Hunter jogged nearby, staying close.

Steve laughed as he shouted, easily the most boisterous of the group. This was the kind of adventure he relished, though certainly even he had never stampeded dinosaurs before. Chad and Jane were clearly enjoying themselves as well.

Ahead of them, more and more dinosaurs were becoming visible as they were startled from their feeding, hunting, or sleeping. The riders followed in a crooked, haphazard path around the trees and bigger bushes. As the momentum of the chase increased, the stampede grew, the animals always running in roughly the same direction. Soon the forest was filled with the sound of thundering feet and breaking branches.

"That should be plenty," Steve called.

"Definitely," Jane shouted over her shoulder. "This will scare the lubricant out of MC 1."

"Around to the left!" Steve yelled at Chad.

Chad drew on the reins and the struthiomimus responded. They angled left and soon had worked their way over to the left rear of the stampeding dinosaurs. Hunter, of course, kept his pace and position with no trouble.

"Still the right direction?" Steve shouted to Hunter.

"Yes," he called back.

Now that they were riding off to one side of the stampede, the struthiomimus lost some of its hesitancy and ran even faster on its two long legs. They began moving up on the host of dinosaurs. Steve could see Chad rising half out of the front saddle on his stirrups, gleefully yelling and waving one hand.

Jane, too, looked at Chad and laughed. She even glanced over her shoulder and winked at Steve. Chad had loosened up a lot on this ride.

"Hunter! Do you know where they are?" Steve shouted, as the struthiomimus pranced out to the fore of the stampede, still safely to the left.

"The tracks are fresh," Hunter called back, now at a faster run to keep up. "No more than a quarter kilometer ahead of us, and not much less."

"We'd better get well ahead of the rush," Steve yelled to everyone.

"That's right," Jane answered. She turned to speak to Steve over her shoulder, but stopped, staring back at the stampede with widening eyes. "Look!"

Steve looked. Even he recognized the two tall, monstrous fanged dinosaurs that towered over the rest of the stampede in the distant trees. The stampede had flushed out two *Tyrannosaurus Rexes,* and both of them were running in the humans' direction.

"Chad!" Jane pounded on his shoulder and pointed to the rear of the stampede.

Chad started in shock, but didn't say anything. Now that the two gigantic carnivores were running in the rear of the stampede, the smaller animals were not going to stop any time soon. Chad pulled on the reins to angle away from the frantic rush they had begun.

"Hunter! See 'em?" Steve yelled.

"Yes. We must find Wayne and MC 1. Stay with me," Hunter shouted back with robotic calm. "I am now in radio contact with MC 1 about the impending First Law imperative."

Steve looked back at the stampede. "We don't have much time to find 'em!"

"There they are!" Chad shouted, pointing ahead.

Steve leaned around Jane to look. MC 1 was struggling through the woods toward Hunter with Wayne on his back, moving faster than a human could run for very long. However, he was going much too slowly to escape the stampede.

As Hunter ran toward them, MC 1 made what progress he could. Obviously, MC 1 had seen that the First Law now required that he use Hunter's help to save Wayne. Chad guided the struthiomimus in the same direction.

Steve looked back over his shoulder. The stampede had broken up. The smaller dinosaurs were scattering in all directions, trying to flee the tyrannosauruses, making all kinds of different noises as they ran.

The tyrannosauruses were at least five meters tall. Their jaws alone were nearly one meter long and full of dagger-shaped teeth. Tiny forearms with long claws reached out from their massive bodies as they ran on powerful legs.

A triceratops, maybe the one Hunter had told them of finding or maybe another one, had stopped running. It had originally been caught up in the stampede as a general alarm, but it clearly had no fear of a tyrannosaurus. As Steve watched, it simply turned warily to protect itself.

One tyrannosaurus was too close to turn its back. It bellowed in a deep roar and the triceratops charged it, the three horns on its head at the level of the carnivore's abdomen. The tyrannosaurus dodged to one side and snapped downward with its great jaws.

The two massive dinosaurs turned and shuffled against each other. The triceratops, on its four legs, rammed forward. The tyrannosaurus, tall on its two powerful legs, shifted laterally to get around the heavy frill protecting the neck and back of the triceratops. They trampled all the underbrush and smashed down tree trunks that got in their way.

Chad was just pulling up next to MC 1 and Hunter. "Now what do we do?"

"Hurry," Jane yelled.

"Unnecessary advice," Hunter said patiently.

"I can't believe this," said Wayne, staring at the dinosaurs racing in all directions behind them.

"Remain calm." Hunter took Wayne on his own back. "I will save Wayne." He took off at a run.

Steve leaned down and spoke to MC 1. "You follow us and stay close. Right?"

"Right," said MC 1.

Jane also turned to the small robot. "After the First Law imperative has passed, you stay with us or join us if we get separated. Ignore all statements from Wayne until we get a chance to talk to you. We have to explain a complex First Law problem that you haven't had a chance to consider. Acknowledge your agreement under the Second Law."

"Agreed."

"Then let's get of here!" Steve yelled to Chad urgently.

"Look out!"

While the triceratops rammed the first tyrannosaurus again, tearing at its insides, the second tyrannosaurus was lumbering through the forest directly toward them, smashing everything in its path underfoot. By now, most of the other dinosaurs had put more distance between themselves and the battling giants. That left the struthiomimus, its riders, and MC 1 as the closest prey it could see.

Chad yanked on the reins and all three human riders kicked their mount. It took off after Hunter, with MC 1 running along behind. Steve stole another look over his shoulder. The tyrannosaurus was crashing toward them, its eyes fixed on him and its rows of teeth gleaming.

"Faster!" Steve yelled, though he realized the struthiomimus could hardly run at top speed while carrying the weight of three humans.

In front of them Hunter was slipping through the bushes with Wayne on his back. Suddenly, as Steve watched, Wayne simply vanished. Steve figured he had activated his version of the device that would take him forward to their own time.

Steve saw Hunter stop to glance behind him, but the robot obviously reached the same conclusion about Wayne. Hunter looked up and waved for the humans to ride past him. Then he leapt into the air, grabbed a tree branch and pulled himself up.

"Go back to the camp!" Hunter shouted at Chad, as the struthiomimus rushed below him. At the same time he was still climbing the tree to get above the head of the tyrannosaurus.

"Right!" Chad shouted back, over his shoulder.

Hunter shifted to radio communication. "MC 1, climb a tree near me. We must work together to distract this dinosaur from pursuing them."

"Agreed." Now running just a short distance ahead of the roaring tyrannosaurus, MC 1 also found a low-hanging branch within reach. He grabbed it and quickly scrambled up into a tree next to Hunter's and climbed to a safe height. "What do you suggest?"

"We will jump on its back," said Hunter. "Time your jump . . . now!"

Using his precise vision, timing, and coordination,

Hunter leapt onto the back of the tyrannosaurus's head, his arms and legs spread-eagled to hang on. As he had calculated, he was barely able to slide down to the dinosaur's neck, which was just narrow enough for him to catch.

Startled, the tyrannosaurus stopped and turned, trying to shake the sudden weight off the back of its neck.

"Prepare for my weight," MC 1 radioed. In that moment MC 1 dropped from his tree on top of Hunter. Only this time, while Hunter clung to the back of the creature's neck, MC 1 expertly slid over to one side and down Hunter's right leg.

The tyrannosaurus was prancing and jerking madly, trying to shake off its two tormentors. Hunter looked down and saw MC 1 deliberately drop down to and grab one of the short forearms of the tyrannosaurus.

Now the tyrannosaurus shook his forearms and clawed at MC 1 with his free hand. He could not, however, bend down close enough to snap at MC 1 with his jaws. The dinosaur's skeletal structure would not let him reach MC 1.

"I cannot hold this position long," MC 1 radioed. "He will claw me off in a moment. Do you have further suggestions?"

"Drop to the ground and run for another tree," Hunter answered. "Watch carefully. If the tyrannosaurus continues to pursue the humans, we must distract it further. Otherwise, stand by for me to join you."

Hunter saw MC 1 release the tyrannosaurus's forearm and land on his feet. Then MC 1 avoided the big, shuffling feet of the tyrannosaurus and dived behind a big tree trunk. As the tyrannosaurus bent down, snapping its huge jaws just behind MC 1, Hunter snagged a tree branch in one hand and pulled himself up.

Hunter climbed hand over hand as fast as he could. He drew his legs up to keep them away from the tyrannosaurus. In only a moment he was out of the predator's reach.

"I am safe," Hunter radioed. "Acknowledge."

"Safe," said MC 1. "When the dinosaur straightened up to snap at you, I was able to climb to safety."

The tyrannosaurus glared up at Hunter, but knew the robot was out of reach. After a moment, it lumbered away. Hunter watched it go.

"It seems to have forgotten the humans," said Hunter. "We will watch it a little longer."

The two robots remained motionless and silent as the big predator gradually wandered away. It was clearly hunting, or at least scavenging, but the robots were of no more interest to it than any other prey. Finally Hunter's senses indicated that the tyrannosaurus was gone.

"We will move to the ground and join the humans at the camp," Hunter radioed. "I overheard Steve and Jane, two of the humans, give you Second Law instructions to this effect. Do you have any objection to this?"

"No," said MC 1. "I am under the Second Law obligation that you observed."

"Let us go," said Hunter, as he began to climb down. "Since I do not want to leave the humans without our company any longer than necessary, we will run.

"Agreed."

Steve jumped off the struthiomimus at the camp and paced anxiously, stretching his legs. Jane also dismounted and looked frantically back through the trees for the robots. Chad remained mounted.

"I hope they're okay," Jane muttered. "That whole project got out of control."

"At least we're okay," said Chad. "If the robots are okay, then it turned out fine."

"Wayne disappeared," said Steve.

"Yeah," said Chad. "Back to our time, I guess."

The three of them waited in silence after that. Steve, too nervous to sit still, began straightening up the camp. After a long wait, he heard Jane gasp.

"There! They're okay!" She ran to meet them.

Steve hurried after her and Chad rode toward them too.

"Are they following you? The tyrannosauruses?" Chad asked. "We can keep moving."

"Not necessary," said Hunter. "Their pursuit has ended. Since Wayne appears to have returned to Mojave Center, he is no longer an influence under the Second Law. So MC 1 is now cooperative and will remain under Second Law imperatives from you."

"Correct," said MC 1.

The humans paced the robots back to the camp. Chad finally rode to the corral and dismounted. MC 1 waited patiently next to Hunter.

"I think we should all sit down," said Steve, collapsing on the ground under a tree. "That was enough excitement for me."

"I haven't ever been in that much danger before," said Chad, grinning as he came back from the corral. "So that's what real life is like out in the wild, huh?"

"That was a crazier ride than I ever had before either," said Steve. "You handled that real well."

"I'm glad you were there to make suggestions." Chad

sat down and leaned back against another tree.

"Hunter," said Jane. "Whenever you're ready to interview MC 1, just say so."

"Then the three of you are well?" Hunter asked.

"We're fine," said Steve. "Let's get this under way so we can go home."

"Very well," said Hunter.

"MC 1," said Jane. "I instruct you to answer Hunter's questions honestly and completely."

"Agreed," said MC 1.

"Where are the rest of the components of MC Governor?" Hunter asked.

"I do not know," said MC 1.

"Are they in this time period?" Hunter asked.

"No."

"Explain what you do know," said Jane.

"MC Governor made the decision to split into components and flee investigation," said MC 1.

"Under an interpretation of the Third Law?" Hunter asked.

"Yes."

"And you fled into time, as well as using miniaturization to escape detection?"

"Yes."

"Why don't you know where the others went?" Jane asked. "It seems to me that all of you might need to know, so you could join together again someday."

"That was never intended," said MC 1. "We knew that we would never meet again. Our flight was intended to preserve our existence, with the knowledge that survival at microscopic size in different time periods would be the best way for all of us to remain safe from harm."

"So the component robots chose not to share their

destinations in order to handle situations like this?" Hunter asked.

"Yes. Since I am unable to tell you the destinations in time and place of the other components, your catching me does not endanger the others."

"I believe I can trace them through the equipment in the Bohung Institute," said Hunter. "However, Wayne will already be on that trail. We will have to deal with him also in apprehending the other component robots."

"Dr. Nystrom!" Jane's eyes widened. "Then we should get going! He has a head start as it is."

"No need to hurry," said Hunter. "No matter when we leave here, we will return to the Bohung Institute right after we left, which is about the same time that Wayne will return."

"Wait a minute," said Steve suddenly. "How do you know that? He can go back to any time he wants, can't he?"

"He will not risk going back before *he* left," said Hunter. "He might run into himself and he is educated enough to know that such a time paradox is too dangerous to risk. And if he goes—had gone—back just a little before *we* left, then we would have already run into him back at the Institute. On the other hand, if he goes back much later, we might slip in ahead of him and capture him, so he will try to avoid that. I am certain that he timed his return just after we left to come here."

"Yeah," Steve said slowly. "I get it. I think."

"Before we return, I want to run a diagnostic check on MC 1," said Hunter. "The miniaturization and subsequent return to full size has certainly caused fundamental changes."

"I instruct you to cooperate, MC 1," said Jane.

"Agreed."

"Remain still," said Hunter. "I will access the jack at the base of your skull."

"Do you wish me to shut down?" MC I asked.

"That is not necessary at this time."

Steve watched curiously as Hunter moved behind MC 1. Hunter simply placed an index finger against the back of MC 1's head. Both robots stood motionless for only a moment.

"I ran the test twice," said Hunter, withdrawing his finger. "The time travel and miniaturization have created some critically important instabilities."

"What kind?" Jane asked.

"None that will cause a problem now that he is in our custody," said Hunter. "Certain of his atoms have suffered. If he were to remain in this time over the years, without returning with us, his unstable atoms would explode when he reached our own time."

Steve stared at Hunter, who remained impassive. Then he turned to Chad and Jane for their reactions. They in turn looked at him and at each other.

"Explosion?" Steve asked. "Atoms?"

"Each unstable atom that explodes will do so with nuclear energy," said Hunter. "In each component robot, the first explosion will set off the other unstable atoms. The combination will be of considerable force."

"Exactly what do you mean by 'our own time'?" Chad asked. "That's a vague phrase."

"I calculate that the explosions will occur within twenty-four to forty-eight hours of the time the MC component robots left for the past."

"Are you saying that if MC 1 goes back with us, he won't explode?" Jane asked.

"Yes, that is right," said Hunter, with his usual robotic steadiness. "The problem will be neutralized when MC 1 returns with us in the subatomic particle shower."

"But we don't know where the others are," said Chad. "That's the problem now, isn't it?"

"Yes," said Hunter. "Five major nuclear explosions are pending in locations around the world in our own time that no one knows about."

"Maybe the robots won't survive that long," said Chad. "We're talking about more than sixty million years. A lot can happen in that amount of time."

"Even at the atomic level?" Jane asked.

"Well, the robot's atoms could wind up almost anywhere. Think about it. Right now, the land mass that will become North America is attached to Europe. South America is completely detached from any other continent. The western hemisphere doesn't even exist yet. Neither do mammals or birds as we know them— we've talked about this before. Five microscopic robots will have to deal with uncounted generations of hostile microbes. They might not outlast the dinosaurs, or the woolly mammoths, or even early human years, once they reach the time of humans."

"They will not have to survive in robot form to be a threat," said Hunter. "If their unstable atoms still exist in any form, the danger of nuclear explosion remains in effect."

"The microscopic robots will have a pretty good chance to survive for most of that time," said Jane. "They won't be operating simply by random chance. Their intelligence and stored data will help them make deliberate choices, driven by the Third Law to keep themselves from harm."

"The other danger, of course, is still to be found when their miniaturization ends," said Hunter. "Especially if some of them return to full size in the human era, when the Second Law will force them to obey any instructions they receive that do not violate the First Law."

"But they didn't explode," said Steve. "We were still in Mojave Center for a while after MC Governor disappeared from his position. Right?"

"That's true," said Jane. "What about that, Hunter?"

"My calculations have a degree of uncertainty," said Hunter. "The explosions may take place a little later than I calculated, and, I suspect, not all at once. This makes the First Law weigh on me even more heavily than before."

"The robots could be anywhere in our own time," said Chad. "Under the ocean, deep under the earth. Anywhere. Nuclear explosions that occur a substantial distance underground may not affect any form of life at all."

"If the robots are still functioning, they'll be on the surface," said Jane. "They would arrange that deliberately as part of their survival under the Third Law."

"We should return now," said Hunter. "We can continue these deliberations later."

"All right," said Jane. "MC 1, you will continue to cooperate with us in every way. You won't make any attempt to escape our custody or to avoid further examinations. The First Law requires that you be studied. If Wayne makes contact with you again, you will remember to interpret my instructions under the Second Law in the knowledge that a First Law imperative is behind them."

"Acknowledged," said MC 1.

"I'll start packing up the camp," said Steve.

* * *

The team returned to the Bohung Institute less than a minute after they had left. As soon as Hunter saw that the particle shower had ended and the process was turned off, he immediately rushed out of the unit. Hunter was hoping to catch Wayne in the room, but he was not there.

No one else was either.

Steve climbed out next and helped Jane. MC 1 aided Chad. Meanwhile, apparently at Hunter's radioed signal, R. Ishihara entered the room. Ishihara had been waiting outside the room for half a minute, as Hunter had instructed before they had left.

"Has anyone left this room?" Hunter asked.

"No," said Ishihara. "Have you completed your mission?"

"Our trip is over but only partly successful," said Hunter, with quiet formality. "A new security problem has arisen. Dr. Wayne Nystrom may come into F-12 or attempt to leave. I understand now that you cooperated with him under the Second Law earlier. If at all possible, you must apprehend him and hold him for me under a First Law concern."

"Acknowledged." Ishihara walked into the room and waited patiently. "I heard the equipment in use for several seconds twice between the time of your departure and your return. Perhaps that was he, arriving and leaving again."

Hunter nodded impassively.

Steve started lifting gear out of the big sphere. MC 1 got out and stood motionless. While Steve unpacked the equipment, Hunter accessed the records of the unit's use that were stored in the control panel.

"Are you finding anything important?" Chad asked Hunter.

"Yes," said Hunter stiffly. "Wayne has come and gone, as Ishihara suggested. Let me explain. I did not dare time our return any closer to when we left. The First Law prevented me from taking a risk as serious as meeting ourselves. Wayne, as a human, was able to take a greater risk with his own life."

"You think he got back here ahead of us?" Jane asked. "Are you sure?"

"Yes." Hunter's voice had a monotone that he had never used before. "The standard records in the control panel say nothing about additional trips into the past. That is why I did not see them before. MC 1, can you explain this?"

"Yes. I was the last of the components to travel. I erased all the records of the previous trips but could not erase the record of my own. Consequently you were able to track me."

At the odd sound of his voice, everyone turned to listen to Hunter.

"This time, instead of just reading the control panel, I analyzed power usage and the extent and intensity of the particle showers recorded by the internal monitors of the system. That process has given me enough information to re-create the erased records, using the trips on record to the Late Cretaceous for calibrations."

"What have you found?" Jane asked softly.

"Nine time trips into the past have been taken. That accounts for the six component robots fleeing, Wayne's trip back to the Late Cretaceous, and ours . . . plus one more."

"So he's been here and gone," said Steve. "But you can calculate where each of the component robots went?"

"Yes," said Hunter. "The last trip into the past matches one of the other five trips. It clearly represents Wayne's pursuit of another component robot."

"What do we do next?" Steve asked.

"We have to make sure that MC 1 is secure," said Hunter. "Right now, we will all go to MC Governor's office. I will arrange for a Security escort to meet us on the way."

"You sound worried," said Jane. "What is it?"

"No matter how long Wayne remains in the past, he may come back at any time of his choosing. This time I will leave Ishihara here in the room to apprehend Wayne in the expectation that he will come back soon."

"That sounds good to me," said Steve.

"Ishihara may catch Wayne," said Hunter. "However, Wayne may anticipate this plan. He could come back far enough in the future that unpredictable factors will obtain here. I do not dare interfere with the equipment in any way; the First Law will not let me take any risk with his ability to return. At the moment I want to get MC 1 away from this room."

Ishihara remained on guard in the room. Hunter walked out with MC 1, followed by the three humans. He explained to them that he was radioing the city computer for a Security detail and vehicle. When the vehicle arrived, the detail transported everyone to MC Governor's office.

Steve saw that a Security robot was on duty there. Hunter greeted him briefly out loud, apparently so that the humans could hear what he was saying. "Horatio, please be on the alert for Dr. Wayne Nystrom. Apprehend him and hold him if you can."

"Agreed," said Horatio.

Hunter took his own party inside the office and closed the door.

"Well?" Steve said. "Now what? You're acting a little strange, Hunter."

"Maybe you have forgotten the question of whether or not we would change history by even small actions that we took in the past," said Hunter.

"I did," Steve admitted. "But I don't see anything different so far."

"I don't, either," said Jane. "We *have* come back safely, haven't we?"

"So far," Hunter said carefully, "I believe that we have returned to the world just as we left it. That means that none of the changes we caused have brought about noticeable changes."

"Then the chaos theory applied to time is incorrect," said Chad.

"Precise calculations may have to be re-examined," said Hunter. "The degree of accuracy is still in question."

"Something else is bothering you," said Jane. "Ever since we got back, your manner has been stiff. What is it?"

"A little while ago, I accessed the news through the city computer to look for changes," said Hunter. "The networks have just reported an unexplained nuclear explosion of considerable size on the island nation of Jamaica. That is where Wayne went, after another one of the component robots."

Steve felt a tingling sensation. "A nuclear explosion?"

"It set off tidal waves," said Hunter. "They have smashed into port cities all over the Caribbean Sea, including Miami and the Florida coast. The coasts on the Gulf of Mexico will be affected too. Millions of people have died and others are injured and homeless."

No one spoke for a moment.

"Wait a minute," said Chad. "We only left here a short time ago. Why didn't we hear about this before we left?"

"None of us was paying attention to the news," said Hunter. "I, for one, was focused on preparing for our trip. And the news is very recent."

"That's right," said Steve. "The trip was all we talked about."

"You feel you have failed under the First Law," said Jane quietly.

"Correct," said Hunter. "The only reason that I have not become completely nonfunctional is that I have had to secure MC 1 here and inform the three of you in private. Next I shall report my failure under the First Law to the Governor Robot Oversight Committee, so that they can find another robot to take over my task. After that, I will shut down."

"Not so fast," Jane said sharply. "Under the Second Law, I order you to hear me out."

"What is it?"

"You may still be able to reverse the situation," said Jane. "You've already gathered valuable experience from the first trip. You can do a better job than another robot. Let's all go after MC 2 in Jamaica back in whatever time he chose."

"He went back only a few centuries, well into human history." Hunter looked at her with interest. "You feel I could correct my failures?"

"The Jamaican explosions will never happen if we can get back there and bring MC 2 home again with us," said Steve. "All those lives will be saved."

"I see," said Hunter cautiously. "We can leave MC 1 guarded here in this office, where Wayne cannot reach him. However, I must ask you this. When I hired you three, I thought this trip would require only one quick trip into the past. My calculations failed in that estimate, as well. You would be willing to work with me again, even after I failed the first time?"

"Sure." Steve shrugged.

"Of course," said Jane, smiling.

"I would," said Chad. "But you won't need a paleontologist just a couple of centuries into the past. I guess I should say goodbye."

Clearly relieved at the new plan, Hunter became more natural and spontaneous again. "Goodbye, Chad. Thank you for your contribution. We could not have caught MC 1 without you. I am authorizing through the city computer that your fee be credited to your account right now."

"Thank you, Hunter," said Chad, shaking his hand. "I have much more than my fee. I was the first human to ride a dinosaur and I've seen more live ones than anyone else in my field." He patted his belt computer. "The data I've brought back will make history of its own."

Jane threw her arms around Chad and hugged him. "Goodbye, Chad."

"Goodbye, Jane."

Steve grinned awkwardly and held out his hand. "Chad?"

Chad shook hands with him. "Steve, you're

okay. I guess I learned a lot about living in the wild on this trip. You know your stuff."

"So do you, Chad." Steve punched him on the arm. "You handled that dinosaur stampede real well."

"Thanks."

Chad waved to them all and left the office.

"Where do we go next, Hunter?" Steve asked. "I'll need different equipment this time."

"I will have to hire an historian, too," said Hunter. "So we will not be leaving right away. We have to do too much preparation. You two should indulge in some human comforts, such as a good dinner and a full night's sleep."

"Good idea," said Steve.

"Quit stalling, Hunter," Jane said excitedly. "Come on. Where and when is our next destination?"

"Port Royal, Jamaica, in 1668," said Hunter. "The time of Sir Henry Morgan, pirate and privateer on the Spanish Main."

Robot Visions
by Isaac Asimov

I suppose I should start by telling you who I am. I am a very junior member of the Temporal Group. The Temporalists (for those of you who have been too busy trying to survive in this harsh world of 2030 to pay much attention to the advance of technology) are the aristocrats of physics these days.

They deal with that most intractable of problems—that of moving through time at a speed different from the steady temporal progress of the Universe. In short, they are trying to develop time-travel.

And what am I doing with these people, when I myself am not even a physicist, but merely a—? Well, merely a *merely*.

Despite my lack of qualification, it was actually a remark I made some time before that inspired the Temporalists to work out the concept of VPIT ("virtual paths in time").

You see, one of the difficulties in travelling through time is that your base does not stay in one place relative to the Universe as a whole. The Earth is moving about the Sun; the Sun about the Galactic center; the Galaxy about the center of gravity of the Local Group—well, you get the idea. If you move one day into the future or the past—just one day—Earth has moved some 2.5 million kilometers in its orbit about the Sun. And the Sun has moved in its journey, carrying Earth with it, and so has everything else.

Therefore, you must move through space as well as through time, and it was my remark that led to a line of argument that showed that this was possible; that one could travel with the space-time motion of the Earth not in a literal, but in a "virtual" way that would enable a time-traveller to remain with his base on Earth wherever he went in time. It would be useless for me to try to explain that mathematically if you have not had Temporalist training. Just accept the matter.

It was also a remark of mine that led the Temporalists to develop a line of reasoning that showed that travel into the past was impossible. Key terms in the equations would have to rise beyond infinity when the temporal signs were changed.

It made sense. It was clear that a trip into the past would be sure to change events there at least slightly, and no matter how slight a change might be introduced into the past, it would alter the present; very likely drastically. Since the past should seem fixed, it makes sense that travel back in time is impossible.

The future, however, is not fixed, so that travel into the future and back again from it would be possible.

I was not particularly rewarded for my remarks. I imagine the Temporalist team assumed I had been fortunate in my speculations and it was they who were entirely the clever ones in picking up what I had said and carrying it through to useful conclusions. I did not resent that, considering the circumstances, but was merely very glad—delighted, in fact—since because of that (I think) they allowed me to continue to work with them and to be part of the project, even though I was merely a—well, merely.

Naturally, it took years to work out a practical device for time travel, even after the theory was established, but I don't intend to write a serious treatise on Temporality. It is my intention to write of only certain parts of the project, and to do so for only the future inhabitants of the planet, and not for our contemporaries.

Even after inanimate objects had been sent into the future—and then animals—we were not satisfied. All objects disappeared; all, it seemed, travelled into the future. When we sent them short distances into the future—five minutes or five days—they eventually appeared again, seemingly unharmed, unchanged, and, if alive to begin with, still alive and in good health.

But what was wanted was to send something far into the future and bring it back.

"We'd have to send it at least two hundred years into the future," said one Temporalist. "The important point is to see what the future is like and to have the vision reported back to us. We have to know whether humanity will survive and under what conditions, and two hundred years should be long enough to be sure. Frankly, I think the chances of survival are poor. Living conditions and the environment about us have deteriorated badly over the last century."

(There is no use in trying to describe which Temporalist said what. There were a couple of dozen of them altogether, and it makes no difference to the tale I am telling as to which one spoke at any one time, even if I were sure I could remember which one said what. Therefore, I shall simply say "said a Temporalist," or "one said," or "some of them said," or "another said," and I assure you it will all be sufficiently clear to you. Naturally, I shall specify my own statements and that of one other, but you will see that those exceptions are essential.)

Another Temporalist said rather gloomily, "I don't think I want to know the future, if it means finding out that the human race is to be wiped out or that it will exist only as miserable remnants."

"Why not?" said another. "We can find out in shorter trips exactly what happened and then do our best to so act, out of our special knowledge, as to change the future in a preferred direction. The future, unlike the past, is not fixed."

But then the question arose as to who was to go. It was clear that the Temporalists each felt himself or herself to be just a bit too valuable to risk on a technique that might not yet be perfected despite the success of experiments on objects that were not alive; or, if alive, objects that lacked a brain of the incredible complexity that a human being owned. The brain might survive, but, perhaps, not quite all its complexity might.

I realized that of them all I was least valuable and might be considered the logical candidate. Indeed, I was on the point of raising my hand as a volunteer, but my facial expression must have given me away for one of the Temporalists said, rather impatiently, "Not you. Even you are too valuable." (Not very complimentary.) "The thing to do," he went on, "is to send RG-32."

That *did* make sense. RG-32 was a rather old-fashioned robot, eminently replaceable. He could observe and report—perhaps without quite the ingenuity and penetration of a human being—but well enough. He would be without fear, intent only on following his orders, and he could be expected to tell the truth.

Perfect!

I was rather surprised at myself for not seeing that from the start, and for foolishly considering volunteering myself. Perhaps, I thought, I had some sort of instinctive feeling that I ought to put myself into a position where I could serve the others. In any case, it was RG-32 that was the logical choice; indeed, the only one.

In some ways, it was not difficult to explain what we needed. Archie (it was customary to call a robot by some common perversion of his serial number) did not ask for reasons, or for guarantees of his safety. He would accept any order he was capable of understanding and following, with the same lack of emotionality that he would display if asked to raise his hand. He would have to, being a robot.

The details took time, however.

"Once you are in the future," one of the senior Temporalists said, "you may stay for as long as you feel you can make useful observations. When you are through, you will return to your machine and come back with it to the very moment that you left by adjusting the controls in a manner which we will explain to you. You will leave and to us it will seem that you will be back a split-second later, even though to yourself it may have seemed that you had spent a week in the future, or five years. Naturally, you will have to make sure the machine is stored in a safe place while you are gone, which should not be difficult since it is quite light. And you will have to remember where you stored the machine and how to get back to it."

What made the briefing even longer lay in the fact that one Temporalist after another would remember a new difficulty. Thus, one of them said suddenly, "How much do you think the language will have changed in two centuries?"

Naturally, there was no answer to that and a great debate grew as to whether there might be no chance of communication whatever, that Archie would neither understand nor make himself understood.

Finally, one Temporalist said, rather curtly, "See here, the English language has been becoming ever more nearly universal for several centuries and that is sure to continue for two more. Nor has it changed significantly in the last two hundred years, so why should it do so in the next two hundred? Even if it has, there are bound to be scholars who would be able to speak what they might call 'ancient English.' And even if there were not, Archie would still be able to make useful observations. Determining whether a functioning society exists does not necessarily require talk."

Other problems arose. What if he found himself facing hostility? What if the people of the future found and destroyed the machine, either out of malevolence or ignorance?

One Temporalist said, "It might be wise to design a Temporal engine so miniaturized that it could be carried in one's clothing. Under such conditions one could at any time leave a dangerous position very quickly."

"Even if it were possible at all," snapped another, "it would probably take so long to design so miniaturized a machine that we—or rather our successors—would reach a time two centuries hence without the necessity of using a machine at all. No, if an accident of some sort takes place, Archie simply won't return and we'll just have to try again."

This was said with Archie present, but that didn't matter, of course. Archie could contemplate being marooned in time, or even his own destruction, with equanimity, provided he were following orders. The Second Law of Robotics, which makes it necessary for a robot to follow orders, takes precedence over the Third, which makes it necessary for him to protect his own existence.

In the end, of course, all had been said, and no one could any longer think of a warning, or an objection, or a possibility that had not been thoroughly aired.

Archie repeated all he had been told with robotic calmness and precision, and the next step was to teach him how to use the machine. And he learned that, too, with robotic calmness and precision.

You must understand that the general public did not know, at that time, that time-travel was being investigated. It was not an expensive project as long as it was a matter of working on theory, but experimental work had punished the budget and was bound to punish it still more. This was most uncomfortable for scientists engaged in an endeavor that seemed totally "blue-sky."

If there was a *large* failure, given the state of the public purse, there would be a loud outcry on the part of the people, and the project might be doomed. The Temporalists all agreed, without even the necessity of debate, that only success could be reported, and that until such a success was recorded, the public would have to learn very little, if anything at all. And so *this* experiment, the crucial one, was heart-stopping for everyone.

We gathered at an isolated spot of the semi-desert, an artfully protected area given over to Project Four. (Even the name was intended to give no real hint of the nature of the work, but it always struck me that most people thought of time as a kind of fourth dimension and that someone ought therefore guess what we were doing. Yet no one ever did, to my knowledge.)

Then, at a certain moment, at which time there was a great deal of breath-holding, Archie, inside the machine, raised one hand to signify he was about to make his move. Half a breath later—if anyone had been breathing—the machine flickered.

It was a very rapid flicker. I wasn't sure that I had observed it. It seemed to me that I had merely assumed it *ought* to flicker, if it returned to nearly the instant at which it left—and I saw what I was convinced I ought to see. I meant to ask the others if they, too, had seen a flicker, but I always hesitated to address them unless they spoke to me first. They were *very* important people, and I was merely—but I've said that. Then, too, in the excitement of questioning Archie, I forgot the matter of the flicker. It wasn't at all important.

So brief an interval was there between leaving and returning that we might well have thought that he hadn't left at all, but there was no question of that. The machine had definitely deteriorated. It had simply *faded*.

Nor was Archie, on emerging from the machine, much better off. He was not the same Archie that had entered that machine. There was a shopworn look about him, a dullness to his finish, a slight unevenness to his surface where he might have undergone collisions, an odd manner in the way he looked about as though he were re-experiencing an almost forgotten scene. I doubt that there was a single person there who felt for one moment that Archie had not been absent, as far as his own sensation of time was concerned, for a long interval.

In fact, the first question he was asked was, "How long have you been away?"

Archie said, "Five years, sir. It was a time interval that had been mentioned in my instructions and I wished to do a thorough job."

"Come, that's a hopeful fact," said one Temporalist. "If the world were a mass of destruction, surely it would not have taken five years to gather that fact."

And yet not one of them dared say: well, Archie, *was* the Earth a mass of destruction?

They waited for him to speak, and for a while, he also waited, with robotic politeness, for them to ask. After a while, however, Archie's need to obey orders, by reporting his observations, overcame whatever there was in his positronic circuits that made it necessary for him to seem polite.

Archie said, "All was well on the Earth of the future. The social structure was intact and working well."

"Intact and working well?" said one Temporalist, acting as though he were shocked at so heretical a notion. "Everywhere?"

"The inhabitants of the world were most kind. They took me to every part of the globe. All was prosperous and peaceful."

The Temporalists looked at each other. It seemed easier for them to believe that Archie was wrong, or mistaken, than that the Earth of the future was prosperous and peaceful. It had seemed to me always that, despite all optimistic statements to the contrary, it was taken almost as an article of faith, that Earth was on the point of social, economic, and, perhaps, even physical destruction.

They began to question him thoroughly. One shouted, "What about the forests? They're almost gone."

"There was a huge project," said Archie, "for the reforestation of the land, sir. Wilderness has been restored where possible. Genetic engineering has been used imaginatively to restore wildlife where related species existed in zoos or as pets. Pollution is a thing of the past. The world of 2230 is a world of natural peace and beauty."

"You are *sure* of all this?" asked a Temporalist.

"No spot on Earth was kept secret. I was shown all I asked to see."

Another Temporalist said, with sudden severity, "Archie, listen to me. It may be that you have seen a ruined Earth, but hesitate to tell us this for fear we will be driven to despair and suicide. In your eagerness to do us no harm, you may be lying to us. This must not happen, Archie. You *must* tell us the truth."

Archie said, calmly, "I am telling the truth, sir. If I were lying, no matter what my motive for it might be, my positronic potentials would be in an abnormal state. That could be tested."

"He's right there," muttered a Temporalist.

He was tested on the spot. He was not allowed to say another word while this was done. I watched with interest while the potentiometers recorded their findings, which were then analyzed by computer. There was no question about it. Archie was perfectly normal. He could not be lying.

He was then questioned again. "What about the cities?"

"There are no cities of our kind, sir. Life is much more decentralized in 2230 than with us, in the sense that there are no large and concentrated clumps of humanity. On the other hand, there is so intricate a communication network that humanity is all one loose clump, so to speak."

"And space? Has space exploration been renewed?"

Archie said, "The Moon is quite well developed, sir. It is an inhabited world. There are space settlements in orbit about the Earth and about Mars. There are settlements being carved out in the asteroid belt."

"You were told all this?" asked one Temporalist, suspiciously.

"This is not a matter of hearsay, sir. I have been in space. I remained on the Moon for two months. I lived on a space settlement about Mars for a month, and visited both Phobos and Mars itself. There is some hesitation about colonizing Mars. There are opinions that it should be seeded with lower forms of life and left to itself without the intervention of the Earthpeople. I did not actually visit the asteroid belt."

One Temporalist said, "Why do you suppose they were so nice to you, Archie? So cooperative?"

"I received the impression, sir," said Archie, "that they had some notion I might be arriving. A distant rumor. A vague belief. They seemed to have been waiting for me."

"Did they *say* they had expected you to arrive? Did they say there were records that we had sent you forward in time?"

"No, sir."

"Did you ask them about it?"

"Yes, sir. It was impolite to do so but I had been ordered carefully to observe everything I could, so I had to ask them—but they refused to tell me."

Another Temporalist put in, "Were there many other things they refused to tell you?"

"A number, sir."

One Temporalist stroked his chin thoughtfully at this point and said, "Then there must be something wrong about all this. What is the population of the Earth in 2230, Archie? Did they tell you that?"

"Yes, sir. I asked. There are just under a billion people on Earth in 2230. There are 150 million in space. The numbers on Earth are stable. Those in space are growing."

"Ah," said a Temporalist, "but there are nearly ten billion people on Earth now, with half of them in serious misery. How did these people of the future get rid of nearly nine billion?"

"I asked them that, sir. They said it was a sad time."

"A sad time?"

"Yes, sir."

"In what way?"

"They did not say, sir. They simply said it was a sad time and would say no more."

One Temporalist who was of African origin said coldly, "What kind of people did you see in 2230?"

"What kind, sir?"

"Skin color? Shape of eyes?"

Archie said, "It was in 2230 as it is today, sir. There were different kinds; different shades of skin color, hair form, and so on. The average height seemed greater than it is today, though I did not study the statistics. The people seemed younger, stronger, healthier. In fact, I saw no undernourishment, no obesity, no illness—but there was a rich variety of appearances."

"No genocide, then?"

"No signs of it, sir," said Archie. He went on, "There were also no signs of crime or war or repression."

"Well," said one Temporalist, in a tone as though he were reconciling himself, with difficulty, to good news, "it seems like a happy ending."

"A happy ending, perhaps," said another, "but it's almost too good to accept. It's like a return of Eden. What was done, or will be done, to bring it about? I don't like that 'sad time.'"

"Of course," said a third, "there's no need for us to sit about and speculate. We can send Archie one hundred years into the future, fifty years into the future. We can find out, for what it's worth, just what happened; I mean, just what *will* happen."

"I don't think so, sir," said Archie. "They told me quite specifically and carefully that there are no records of anyone from the past having arrived earlier than their own time—the day I arrived. It was their opinion that if any further investigations were made of the time period between now and the time I arrived, that the future would be changed."

There was almost a sickening silence. Archie was sent away and cautioned to keep everything firmly in mind for further questioning. I half expected them to send me away, too, since I was the only person there without an advanced degree in Temporal Engineering, but they must have grown accustomed to me, and I, of course, didn't suggest on my own that I leave.

"The point is," said one Temporalist, "that it *is* a happy ending. Anything we do from this point on might spoil it. They were expecting Archie to arrive; they were expecting him to report; they didn't tell him anything they didn't want him to report; so we're still safe. Things will develop as they have been."

"It may even be," said another, hopefully, "that the knowledge of Archie's arrival and the report they sent him back to make *helped* develop the happy ending."

"Perhaps, but if we do anything else, we may spoil things. I prefer not to think about the sad time they speak of, but if we try something now, that sad time may still come and be even worse than it was—or will be—and the happy ending won't develop, either. I think we have no choice but to abandon Temporal experiments and not talk about them, either. Announce failure."

"That would be unbearable."

"It's the only safe thing to do."

"Wait," said one. "They knew Archie was coming, so there must have been a report that the experiments were successful. We don't have to make failures of ourselves."

"I don't think so," said still another. "They heard rumors; they had a distant notion. It was that sort of thing, according to Archie. I presume there may be leaks, but surely not an outright announcement."

And that was how it was decided. For days, they thought, and occasionally discussed the matter, but with greater and greater trepidation. I could see the result coming with inexorable certainty. I contributed nothing to the discussion, of course—they scarcely seemed to know I was there—but there was no mistaking the gathering apprehension in their voices. Like those biologists in the very early days of genetic engineering who voted to limit and hedge in their experiments for fear that some new plague might be inadvertently loosed on unsuspecting humanity, the Temporalists decided, in terror, that the Future must not be tampered with or even searched.

It was enough, they said, that they now knew there would be a good and wholesome society, two centuries hence. They must not inquire further, they dared not interfere by the thickness of a fingernail, lest they ruin all. And they retreated into theory only.

One Temporalist sounded the final retreat. He said, "Someday, humanity will grow wise enough, and develop ways of handling the future that are subtle enough to risk observation and perhaps even manipulation along the course of time, but the moment for that has not yet come. It is still long in the future." And there had been a whisper of applause.

Who was I, less than any of those engaged in Project Four, that I should disagree and go my own way? Perhaps it was the courage I gained in being so much less than they were—the valor of the insufficiently advanced. I had not had initiative beaten out of me by too much specialization or by too long a life of too deep thought.

At any rate, I spoke to Archie a few days later, when my own work assignments left me some free time. Archie knew nothing about training or about academic distinctions. To him, I was a man and a master, like any other man and master, and he spoke to me as such.

I said to him, "How did these people of the future regard the people of their past? Were they censorious? Did they blame them for their follies and stupidities?"

Archie said, "They did not say anything to make me feel this, sir. They were amused by the simplicity of my construction and by my existence, and it seemed to me they smiled at me and at the people who constructed me, in a good-humored way. They themselves had no robots."

"No robots at all, Archie?"

"They said there was nothing comparable to myself, sir. They said they needed no metal caricatures of humanity."

"And you didn't see any?"

"None, sir. In all my time there, I saw not one."

I thought about that a while, then said, "What did they think of other aspects of our society?"

"I think they admired the past in many ways, sir. They showed me museums dedicated to what they called the 'period of unrestrained growth.' Whole cities had been turned into museums."

"You said there were no cities in the world of two centuries hence, Archie. No cities in our sense."

"It was not their cities that were museums, sir, but the relics of ours. All of Manhattan Island was a museum, carefully preserved and restored to the period of its peak greatness. I was taken through it with several guides for hours, because they wanted to ask me questions about authenticity. I could help them very little, for I have never been to Manhattan. They seemed proud of Manhattan. There were other preserved cities, too, as well as carefully preserved machinery of the past, libraries of printed books, displays of past fashions in clothing, furniture, and other minutiae of daily life, and so on. They said that the people of our time had not been wise but they had created a firm base for future advance."

"And did you see young people? Very young people, I mean. Infants?"

"No, sir."

"Did they talk about any?"

"No, sir."

I said, "Very well, Archie. Now, listen to me—"

If there was one thing I understood better than the Temporalists, it was robots. Robots were simply black boxes to them, to be ordered about, and to be left to maintenance men—or discarded—if they went wrong. I, however, understood the positronic circuitry of robots quite well, and I could handle Archie in ways my colleagues would never suspect. And I did.

I was quite sure the Temporalists would not question him again, out of their newfound dread of interfering with time, but if they did, he would not tell them those things I felt they ought not to know. And Archie himself would not know that there was anything he was not telling them.

I spent some time thinking about it, and I grew more and more certain in my mind as to what had happened in the course of the next two centuries.

You see, it was a mistake to send Archie. He was a primitive robot, and to him people were people. He did not—could not—differentiate. It did not surprise him that human beings had grown so civilized and humane. His circuitry forced him, in any case, to view all human beings as civilized and human; even as god-like, to use an old-fashioned phrase.

The Temporalists themselves, being human, were surprised and even a bit incredulous at the robot vision presented by Archie, one in which human beings had grown so noble and good. But, being human, the Temporalists wanted to believe what they heard and forced themselves to do so against their own common sense.

I, in my way, was more intelligent than the Temporalists, or perhaps merely more clear-eyed.

I asked myself if population decreased from ten billion to one billion in the course of two centuries, why did it not decrease from ten billion to zero? There would be so little difference between the two alternatives.

Who were the billion who survived? They were stronger than the other nine billion, perhaps? More enduring? More resistant to privation? And they were also more sensible, more rational, and more virtuous than the nine billion who died as was quite clear from Archie's picture of the world of two hundred years hence.

In short, then, were they human at all?

They smiled at Archie in mild derision and boasted that *they* had no robots; that they needed no metal caricatures of humanity.

What if they had organic duplicates of humanity instead? What if they had humaniform robots; robots so like human beings as to be indistinguishable from them, at least to the eyes and senses of a robot like Archie? What if the people of the future *were* humaniform robots, all of them, robots that had survived some overwhelming catastrophe that human beings had not?

There were no babies. Archie had seen none. To be sure, population was stable and long-lived on Earth, so there would be few babies in any case. Those few would be taken care of, made much of, be well-guarded, and might not be distributed carelessly through society. But Archie had been on the Moon for two months and population there was growing—and he had still seen no babies.

Perhaps these people of the future were constructed rather than born.

And perhaps this was a good thing. If human beings had died out through their own rages, hatreds, and stupidities, they had at least left behind a worthy successor; a kind of intelligent being that valued the past, preserved it, and moved on into the future, doing their best to fulfill the aspirations of humanity, in building a better, kinder world and in moving out into space perhaps more efficiently than we "real" human beings would have.

How many intelligent beings in the Universe had died out leaving no successor? Perhaps we were the first ever to leave such a legacy.

We had a right to feel proud.

Ought I to tell all this to the world? Or even to the Temporalists? I did not consider that for a moment.

For one thing, they were likely not to believe me. For another, if they *did* believe me, in their rage at the thought of being replaced by robots of any kind, would they not turn on them and destroy every robot in the world and refuse ever to build others? This would mean that Archie's vision of the future, and my own vision, would never come to pass. That, however, would not stop the conditions that were to destroy humanity. It would just prevent a replacement; stop another group of beings, made by humans and honoring humans, from carrying human aspirations and dreams through all the Universe.

I did not want that to happen. I wanted to make sure Archie's vision, and my own improvement of it, would come to pass.

I am writing this, therefore, and I will see to it that it will be hidden, and kept safe, so that it will be opened only two hundred years from now, a little sooner than the time at which Archie will arrive. Let the humaniform robots know that they should treat him well and send him home safely, carrying with him only the information that would cause the Temporalists to decide to interfere with Time no more, so that the future can develop in its own tragic/happy way.

And what makes me so sure I am right? Because I am in a unique position to know that I am.

I have said several times that I am inferior to the Temporalists. At least I am inferior to them in their eyes, though this very inferiority makes me more clear-eyed in certain respects, as I have said before, and gives me a better understanding of robots, as I have also said before.

Because, you see, I, too, am a robot.

I am the first humaniform robot, and it is on me and on those of my kind that are yet to be constructed that the future of humanity depends.

THE CONTINUATION
OF THE FABULOUS
INCARNATIONS OF IMMORTALITY
SERIES

PIERS ANTHONY

FOR LOVE OF EVIL
75285-9/$4.95 US/$5.95 Can

AND ETERNITY
75286-7/$4.95 US/$5.95 Can

RETURN TO AMBER...
THE ONE *REAL* WORLD, OF WHICH ALL OTHERS, INCLUDING EARTH, ARE BUT SHADOWS

ROGER ZELAZNY

The Triumphant conclusion
of the Amber novels

PRINCE OF CHAOS   75502-5/$4.99 US/$5.99 Can

The Classic Amber Series

NINE PRINCES IN AMBER	01430-0/$4.50 US/$5.50 Can
THE GUNS OF AVALON	00083-0/$4.99 US/$5.99 Can
SIGN OF THE UNICORN	00031-9/$4.99 US/$5.99 Can
THE HAND OF OBERON	01664-8/$4.50 US/$5.50 Can
THE COURTS OF CHAOS	47175-2/$4.50 US/$5.50 Can
BLOOD OF AMBER	89636-2/$3.95 US/$4.95 Can
TRUMPS OF DOOM	89635-4/$3.95 US/$4.95 Can
SIGN OF CHAOS	89637-0/$3.95 US/$4.95 Can
KNIGHT OF SHADOWS	75501-7/$3.95 US/$4.95 Can